CW00541395

The Blandford School

Catalogue: 04087

BLACK NOVEMBER

BLACK NOVEMBER

by

Rex Harley

LONDON
VICTOR GOLLANCZ LTD
1988

First published in Great Britain 1988
by Victor Gollancz Ltd,
14 Henrietta Street, London WC2E 8QJ

British Library Cataloguing in Publication Data
Harley, Rex
  Black november.
  I. Title
  823'.914[F]   PZ7

ISBN 0-575-04150-1

Typeset at The Spartan Press Ltd,
Lymington, Hants
and printed in Great Britain by
St Edmundsbury Press Ltd, Bury St Edmunds, Suffolk.

In memoriam
Wardell Gray
1921–1955

Chapter One

The young man opens the case and smiles at the curved instrument in its velvet bed. Cupping the mouthpiece in his hands he blows into the reed, coaxing it to warmth and life. He fixes it in place, puts the saxophone to his lips, works the keys with his fingers. Inside, a column of air vibrates without note. He knows well the virtues of patience. Give it time; time to link itself to your fingers and breath, so you both speak with the same voice. And when the time is right — no wavering. Push the first notes hard. That way they're born strong and healthy.

The music bursts into the sunlit room, slicing, weaving, floating round the solitary musician. Listening to the song of the saxophone he catches a phrase, draws it out and lets it lead him on.

Stuart is standing in the doorway. He has crept up to the second floor, called by the music of the Black man standing near the window. The man's back is turned to Stuart. His eyes are closed in concentration, and against the sun which slants through the glass on to his body. For a moment he appears to be a vision of pure colour: red sweatshirt, saxophone flashing golden in the warm light.

When the song has run its course he stops, cradles the instrument in his arms and exhales deeply. Finally he turns and a wide grin appears on his face.

"A secret audience, huh? Didn't realise you liked jazz."

"Me?" Stuart shrugs his shoulders, embarrassed now. "Not thought about it really. Just heard you playing so I thought — "

"Not disturbing you, was I?"

"No — just checking. See if you're OK."

"Fine, thanks. Couldn't be better. Having a place to practise makes one hell of a difference. My landlady's not so tolerant. Reckons all music is anti-social. And I can't afford to lose my digs. They're cheap and I'm poor so we suit each other pretty well. That reminds me. How much do I owe you for the use of the room?"

Stuart shakes his head. "'s all right, Calvin. Jarrod's a friend. And any friend of his — "

Calvin holds up a hand to interrupt. "Not a friend exactly. I just know him, from the club. We happened to be talking one night — I believe in talking to the bouncer: you never know when you might need him."

"It's OK. The room's empty. You need a place to practise. No money. All right?"

"Thanks." Calvin smiles.

"Anyhow, I'll leave you to it." Stuart closes the door and goes downstairs. Nice enough bloke, he thinks. 'Any friend of Jarrod's!' He and Jarrod have never been friends, but when someone weighing eighteen stones asks for a favour it's a brave man who says no; and bravery isn't one of Stuart's more notable qualities.

For half an hour he occupies himself with small jobs in the messy kitchen before climbing the stairs once more. This time he stops on the first floor landing, takes out a small bunch of keys and opens a door at the back, behind the stairwell. It leads to a large room which contains a single table and six upright chairs. He opens the window (the first time it has been touched for a month), fusses briefly with the chairs, straightening a couple of them, then locks the room again. Music is still drifting gently down the stairs.

Back in the kitchen he opens a beer.

An hour passes. There is a knock at the kitchen door and Calvin's face appears. "I'm off now."

"Fancy a drink before you go?" Stuart nods towards a stack of cans on the table.

"Thanks, but I'd better not. Drinking at this time of day makes me sleepy, and I really ought to put in an appearance at college. Slap a bit of paint on a canvas."

"You don't sound too keen."

"Oh, it's OK — when I'm in the mood. Just that some things are more important right now."

"Playing at the club?"

Calvin grins conspiratorially. "That and other things!"

"You're a dark horse, aren't you? I mean — "

Calvin suddenly throws back his head and roars with laughter. "White people get embarrassed so easily," he chortles. "And your blushes show up more too. See you."

When he has finished his beer Stuart returns to the first floor room to close the window. The place is aired and ready.

It is later. Stuart is downstairs letting in the guests. There are two of them. The older man is smartly dressed and carrying a briefcase. Stuart nods respectfully in his direction.

"Evening, Mr Schaeffer."

"Evening, Stuart."

Outside the door, hovering on the edge of brightness cast by the hall light, is a younger man.

"Perhaps you'd better leave us, Stuart. Wait in the kitchen or something. Our friend here has an understandable desire for anonymity."

"Yes, Mr Schaeffer."

The older man leans forward, a disapproving frown creasing his well-shaven face. "Been drinking, Stuart?"

"Well, just — "

"Maybe you'd prefer to go out for a while. Walk around a bit. Sober up."

Stuart nods agreement and leaves, taking care not to turn his head as he passes the visitor on the path. As he opens the gate he can hear the front door shutting.

The surrounding streets are quiet. Stuart stops on a corner to light a cigarette. He has not been told what the meeting is about, but he can guess. Mr Schaeffer has contacts everywhere: can provide anything for anyone, if the price is right.

Over his head the sky hangs vast and ragged. Torn clouds scud across the moon and drape themselves over whole clusters of stars. A wild night. Twice Stuart walks slowly round the block before re-entering the house. The cold air has made him light-headed and he is not prepared for what greets him when he opens the kitchen door.

"Hi."

Calvin is sitting at the kitchen table.

"Well, aren't you going to say hello? Offer me a drink even? I won't say no this time."

"How did you — ?"

"You left the front door unlocked. Thought I'd give you a

surprise but you weren't here. Got something for you to listen to." He leans forward and Stuart notices the portable tape deck on the table. Calvin presses a button and music floods the room. "Recorded yesterday at the club," he explains loudly. "What do you think?"

Everything has happened too fast for Stuart. He is frozen: legs and voice.

"Going to send it to a record company," Calvin continues blithely. "That's why I need a place to practise. Anyway, you have a listen to it. I'll be back in a minute."

Before Stuart can stop him he is out in the hallway. "Saxophone," he calls back over his shoulder. "Left it here this morning, ready for tomorrow. If you like, I can play a duet with myself. Hang about."

Stuart rushes after him, but he is taking the stairs two at a time. His feet are already pounding on the second flight as Stuart reaches the first landing. The door opens. Mr Schaeffer stands framed by the light from the room. "What the hell — ?" he says, and now Calvin has got the case and is starting the downward journey. Stuart turns his head to stare in panic as Calvin's legs come into view. Then they are together, the three of them on the landing. Over Mr Schaeffer's shoulder another figure appears.

"Hi," Calvin says cheerfully.

Chapter Two

Light beamed through each pane of glass in the third floor window and, very faintly, music filtered down to street level. There were no passers-by to hear it and most of the other windows in the street were dark. Rising above the silent houses, Number twenty-nine had become a lighthouse in a sea of dull brick and slate. It was Sunday; half-past midnight.

At the bottom of Calvin's wastepaper bin a pile of empty lager cans was accumulating. Calvin was sitting in the centre of the room on a piece of foam-backed carpet, an off-cut bought cheap from the market. He lobbed another can in the direction of the bin. It bounced off the edge and clattered over the floorboards, finally coming to rest up against the far skirting board.

He had to admit, the tape was good. Despite being recorded on a small machine propped on one of the tables in the club the sound was quite acceptable — clear enough to give the recording company some idea of what he could do. They didn't expect miracles and, after all, he wouldn't be going to them in the first place if he had decent recording facilities of his own. At least they'd expressed an interest. That was promising in itself. Unlike pop music, no-one stood to make a fortune out of jazz.

He was so engrossed in his thoughts that he failed to notice the tape had ended until the machine automatically clicked off. He rubbed his hand across his eyes. Time to sober up, to leave the comparative comfort of his small electric fire and venture down to the kitchen to make a cup of coffee. He groaned inwardly and rose, a little unsteadily, to his feet.

Making his way carefully down the wooden stairs to the next floor he found the light switch before continuing his trek to the kitchen. He filled the old aluminium kettle and placed it on the gas. The place was freezing. Suddenly aware of just how much lager he had drunk, he climbed back upstairs to the shabby bathroom.

It was as cold as the kitchen and he shivered involuntarily. A cloud of steam rose from the lavatory. One day, he thought, I shall live in a house with central heating. No more shaking and shivering, or huddling over the two orange bars of an ancient fire.

He flushed the toilet and stepped back on to the landing. There was an unearthly silence here, a no-man's land of carpets and candy stripes. Just over a week he'd been here but in all that time, apart from occasional glimpses of Stuart in or around the kitchen, and the brief meeting with Stuart's odd friends, he'd not seen a soul. No-one had emerged from the freshly painted doors on the first floor again. They had remained firmly closed. Closed . . . and locked? Calvin had no idea and, until now, no curiosity.

There were three doors: two in the long wall at the front of the building and one next to the bathroom at the rear. Calvin padded over to this last door and stood quietly listening. No sound. And no light from underneath. Making as little noise as possible he reached down to the round, old-fashioned doorknob and twisted it clockwise. The door remained shut. He turned it the other way and pushed again. When nothing happened he didn't know whether to feel disappointed or relieved. His thoughts were interrupted by a shrill whistle. The kettle. He'd nearly forgotten.

Five minutes later he was back in his own room. It wasn't a palace, certainly, but he wasn't complaining. In a strange sort of way it was actually beginning to feel like home.

To the accompanying creak of a stray bed-spring Calvin stretched under his heavy blanket and reluctantly opened his eyes. The window was beaded with condensation, through which a lemon dawn glared into the room. He checked his watch: seven-thirty. No point in trying to get back to sleep now, but he was unwilling to step out into the world. He poked one foot experimentally beyond the bottom of the bed like a horizontal swimmer testing the water, and groaned. Would it be easier in stages or should he make a sudden leap to his bundle of clothes and get dressed as quickly as possible? He lay for another minute, debating.

"OK," he said at last, and whipped back the blanket. The accumulated cold air of the night swallowed him up before he could reach the clothes. Hastily he threw on underwear, jeans and a large grey sweatshirt with *Bebop* emblazoned in red on the chest. He rubbed his hands together vigorously and breathed on the tips of his fingers.

Would he disturb anyone if he practised for a while before making himself a pot of tea? It seemed unlikely. His room was level with the roof of the house next door — no-one to disturb there — and Stuart was unlikely to hear him from the basement.

He pulled the black case from under the bed and removed the instrument. Within a minute the ballad he had been listening to the previous night burst into the crisp morning, slicing, weaving and finally floating around the figure seated on the bed. Listening to the song of the saxophone Calvin caught a phrase, drew it out and let it lead him on. His eyes were closed in concentration and against the sun, which slanted through the glass and hit the right side of his body. The saxophone flashed golden.

After a few minutes he stopped and, cradling the instrument in his lap, exhaled deeply. Downstairs he heard the front door bang. He moved over to the window and wiped a pane of glass clear with his fist. Stuart was just closing the front gate. He's up early today, Calvin thought: the sun must have woken him as well.

Calvin ran his tongue round dry lips. He could murder a cup of tea.

The soft carpeting of the first floor felt warm beneath his feet. It would be so much more convenient to have a room down here. Maybe, if they were not being used, he could persuade Stuart to let him move. Well, he'd tried one door and that hadn't yielded much, except a solid lock and a slight feeling of guilt on his part. Why feel guilty, though? It was hardly a crime. He stood for a moment, picturing Stuart as he set off up the road, then made up his mind.

Just because one had been locked, that didn't mean they all were. He moved to the door facing the stairs and turned the doorknob. With no extra pressure at all the door swung gently open. Through the opening Calvin could see a large chunk of floral wallpaper, but nothing else.

Suddenly he stopped. He had been about to push the door open further when the thought struck him. He was assuming, simply on the basis of seeing no-one else in the house,

15

that the room was empty. But it was equally possible that he would burst in on some unsuspecting sleeper and scare him half to death.

There was only one way of checking. He tapped on the glossy wood, gently at first then louder. There was no reply. Pushing the door back as far as it would go, he stepped into the room.

What caught Calvin's eye immediately was the small washbasin in the corner: toothbrush holder, upturned glass tumbler on a shelf below the mirror. And over the mirror itself was a small fluorescent light-fitting complete with shaving socket: the sort of thing you usually found only in a boarding house or small hotel.

The room itself was comfortably furnished and the bedside table had that same air of having been transported from a hotel: reading lamp, small empty shelves level with the headboard of the bed. But it was the bed itself that made Calvin's brow furrow in a questioning frown. For not only was it carefully made, but the sheets and blankets had been folded back at the top in a neat diagonal, rather like the first step in the making of a paper aeroplane.

He turned to the wardrobe. There was nothing inside it.

He had been right, but only in part. No-one else was staying in the house at the moment. Equally clearly, someone was expected; someone who, unlike Calvin, merited the comfort and convenience of the first floor.

The two men in the car barely knew each other. Their conversation, breaking long periods of silence, was functional.

"This safe-house of yours — "

"I prefer to think of it as a guest house; it sounds more . . . conventional."

"All legal and above board, huh?"

"Hardly legal."

"But safe?"

"Certainly. 'Anonymity Hall' you might say."

"And the caretaker? How much does he know?"

"That you're arriving today, you'll be staying for two days at the most and that he's to leave you to your own devices."

"But he doesn't know who I am?"

"No."

"Or what I am?"

"You mean a business acquaintance of mine, or an international thug on the run?"

The other man continued to stare at the view beyond the windscreen but his voice hardened. "You prefer 'guest house'," he said tersely. "I prefer 'dealer in arms'."

"Apologies. Stuart is merely aware that you are evading the forces of law and order. All our guests are in the same position."

A note of panic entered the other man's voice. "There's no-one else there at the moment?"

"No, no. There hasn't been anyone else there for — oh, six months at least."

The man relaxed. Having secured his own position, the conversation ceased. He leaned forward and pushed the cigar lighter on the dashboard. The wire element inside began to glow orange as the car eased off the ring road and into secluded back streets. There was a click and the lighter was ready. The man lit a cigarette and blew smoke against the windscreen.

"This Stuart," he said at last. "Are you saying he gets paid for looking after an empty house?"

"More than looking after it. Technically speaking, he's the owner too."

"So no-one can tie it to you?"

"Exactly."

"You don't take many risks do you, Mr Schaeffer?"

"Indeed I don't, and that makes things safer for you, too."

"I know. It was intended as a compliment."

Silence again fell upon the car till it pulled to a stop a few minutes later.

"The house is down that road there, about two-thirds of the way along. Number twenty-nine. I think it wiser if I drop you here, though."

The other man smiled. "Of course."

He withdrew a fat envelope from the inside of his coat and handed it to the driver. Mr Schaeffer pulled out the wad of notes and flipped expertly through it like a card dealer fast-shuffling.

"Fine. A pleasure doing business with you. I hope you enjoy your stay."

The man climbed out of the passenger seat and removed a small suitcase from the back.

"The quieter the better," he said, and set off down the street.

Calvin was approaching the long iron footbridge over the railway. Around him, leaves that had clung tenaciously to winter branches were now piled in small drifts or pressed against fences by the wind. The path up to the bridge began with a tubular railing, waist-height and shaped like an enormous croquet hoop. He gripped the cold metal with both hands, balanced his weight on his hips, then leaned forward and spun round: a human Catherine wheel. Blood rushed to his head. Perhaps gymnastics was not the best activity after several pints with his friends in the student bar. When they'd found out his good news about the recording company the evening had rapidly turned into a major celebration.

The footpath sloped up, bringing it level with the roofs of the storage sheds in the sidings below. The narrow bridge itself had heavy riveted metal plates in its floor and the sides were plastered with spray-paint slogans: many crude, some hateful and others plain ridiculous. When people walked across, every step produced a clanking echo that reverberated from one end to the other. Calvin decided to sprint. As he gathered speed the soles of his feet drummed on the bridge and the painted slogans blurred together, a chaos of jumbled words.

Once over, he stopped to catch his breath then cut across the grass of a small park on his left. On the far side was the entry to an alley he'd discovered recently, which saved a quarter of a mile's extra walking. It ran between high walls that kept the large gardens on either side strictly private. The tops of tall trees at the bottom of the gardens peered over the wall, but no passer-by could look in.

The entry was unlit and no-one but the young used it after dark; if anyone was lurking halfway down, perhaps a small group of bored youths bent on some violent fun and easy money, they would not be seen. Once encountered there would be no retreat and, shout as loud as you might, the thick, high walls would bounce your cry for help mockingly back.

The first streetlight at the end of the alleyway came more clearly into view. A frail finger of light wavered between the leaning walls, illuminating a patch of leaf-strewn ground. Calvin emerged on to the pavement. The house was now only a short walk away. He slowed to a comfortable stroll.

Outside the house he stopped. A light was on, up in the first floor bedroom. So, the new arrival was installed. Maybe he should pop his head in on the way upstairs and say hello. He turned into the passage, ran down the basement steps to the peeling, grey door and let himself in. As he walked past Stuart's door it suddenly opened and Stuart stepped in front of him. Even in the half-light of the hallway Calvin could see the tension on his face.

"Where have you been all day?" Stuart asked. "I went up to your room this morning but you'd already gone."

"Yeah. I woke up early, same as you, so I left early. What's the problem?"

By way of answer, Stuart took hold of his shoulder and tried to steer him into the downstairs room. "Hey!" Calvin raised his voice. "What the hell are you doing?"

Stuart hastily let go and cast an anxious glance towards the staircase. "I just want to talk to you a minute. It's important."

Calvin was not in the mood to be pushed around. He stood where he was. "OK. Tell me here," he said.

"All right, have it your own way. I wanted to tell you this morning . . . You've got to leave."

Calvin stared at him, speechless. "You *what*?" he said

inally. "I've only been here a week. What've I done to get lung out?"

"You haven't done anything. I made a mistake, that's all. Here." He stepped back into the doorway. "I've got your suitcase and your tape deck. I'm sorry but you'll have to leave now."

Calvin shook his head. "I don't believe this."

"Please," Stuart begged him. "Just go."

"So where's the sax?" Calvin asked quietly, fighting to control his anger.

"What?"

"The saxophone! Or have you nicked it, huh?"

"I thought you'd . . . " Stuart began, but before he could finish the sentence Calvin had thrust past him and was bounding up the stairs. "No, wait," Stuart shouted after him.

Calvin reached the first landing then crashed up the wooden staircase to the top of the house and into his room. What the hell did that guy think he was playing at? Bundling his things together and trying to push him out into the night like some vagrant.

He lifted the edge of the blanket from where it had draped itself on to the floor, and felt underneath the bed. The saxophone was still there; Stuart must have missed seeing it. And there on the top was the cassette in its box. He pulled the case out and was about to slip the cassette into his pocket when Stuart burst through the door.

He grabbed at Calvin and for a moment the two of them tussled in the centre of the room. As they fought the plastic box fell from Calvin's hand and crashed to the floor, scattering its contents. Calvin broke loose and braced himself for a further onslaught but Stuart merely stood there, breathing hard.

"Get out of here," he grated. "For God's sake."

"Why?" Calvin shot at him. He thought of the carefully made bed downstairs, the light at the window and Stuart' panic-stricken glance up the stairs. "Of course," he said slowly. "This is all to do with your new arrival, isn't it?"

Stuart's eyes met his and Calvin looked at them in horror. The man was terrified. Like a startled rabbit, he was frozen to the spot. What was this all about? There was only one way to know for certain. Calvin ran back out of the room and down to the first floor. Without knocking he threw open the bedroom door.

The man was standing facing the window. The curtains were closed; he was staring at nothing in particular. His stillness brought Calvin to an abrupt halt. He stood in the doorway and waited. Behind him he could hear Stuart coming down the stairs. Still the man did not move.

But Calvin was not going to back off now. "Who are you?" he demanded. "What are you doing here?" He took one step closer to the motionless figure.

The man by the window turned slowly, but it was not his face that Calvin saw; it was the barrel of a gun, and the large canister on the end was pointing towards him. He opened his mouth to speak again and the gun thudded. Calvin was pushed backwards by an enormous pressure in his chest.

For a second he hovered in the open doorway, then his head tipped forward, as if to examine the hole that had been drilled expertly into his heart, and his legs folded beneath him.

Over his dying figure, the man spoke to the shaken caretaker. "You've made a nasty mess of things," he said. "Now go downstairs and phone Mr Schaeffer."

The cassette box lay on the floor where it had fallen. As he paced the room Mr Schaeffer's foot stubbed against it. He picked the box up and threw it on the bed. "So this is where he was living," he said. "The place is a tip. It'll need sorting out — after we've dealt with the other matter."

The three men walked back down to the first floor, Mr Schaeffer looked at the body, then over to Stuart. When he spoke the words spat from his mouth like tiny slivers of shrapnel.

"You stupid bastard."

He turned away from the corpse and his gaze met that of the third man. He was the only one who seemed unperturbed by events.

"The buck stops with you, Mr Schaeffer," he said calmly. "That's what you get your money for: ultimate responsibility."

Mr Schaeffer made no reply. Turning to the man who had placed him in his present predicament he said, "Time is not on our side, Stuart. I shan't go into all the details with you now, but I presume you committed this piece of imbecility so you could make a few extra pennies on the side."

Stuart was not fooled by the gentle tone of the voice. "I didn't think you'd need the house again so soon, honest . . . "

"No, you didn't think. Tell me, Stuart, when do you ever? I seem to remember *him*" — he indicated the corpse — "one evening not very long ago. Here in this house. A friend of yours, you said. Just visiting, you said. And I was foolish enough to believe you."

"I'm sorry."

"And now I find," Mr Schaeffer continued, each word hard as a slap in the face, "that you've let him move in — bed and all!"

"He only slept here a couple of times. He liked to practise late at night, so I let him . . . " He tailed off helplessly, his arms at his side and his head lowered in acknowledgement of his stupidity. Mr Schaeffer took a step closer.

"Look at me, Stuart."

Stuart raised his head to look at the cold, venomous eyes of his employer. He did not see the fist that planted itself unerringly in his solar plexus, doubling him up with pain. As he fought to regain his breath, Mr Schaeffer turned to the other man.

"As you say, I take ultimate responsibility, but others must suffer a little for their carelessness." He helped Stuart to his feet again as if nothing had passed between them. It was a gesture of pure pantomime.

"Come along, Stuart. There's work to be done. First we dispose of the body, then we'll sort out his belongings. No doubt by now someone will know he's been living here so there's bound to be enquiries. You say he seemed drunk when he came in?"

"Yes he was . . . " Stuart gasped. "I could smell it . . . on his breath."

Mr Schaeffer reflected on this. "So he was out for the evening — with some friends, say. He left them and walked back here. Pity it's a bullet wound or we could have made out he was attacked on the way home and dumped the body for someone to find it. Looks like he'll just have to disappear. We'll sort out the finer points later, but drunks are notoriously argumentative. So, let's say he came round here drunk; turned nasty; you told him he'd better leave or you'd call the police, and off he went in a violent temper taking all his stuff with him. So long as there's no body there's no evidence. Once we've got the story sorted out you just stick to it."

He patted the despondent man gently on the shoulder. "Cheer up, Stuart. Everything's going to be fine."

Chapter Three

The board over the shop door announced *Appleby's Antiques. Curios and Second Hand Furniture.* Simon stood on the opposite side of the road. He looked up and down the long street of old terraced houses that stretched away on either side of the shop. There was no-one around; no-one to ask directions from. If he was ever going to find his way to the swimming baths he would have to ask in the antique shop.

If only he'd got on the bus from the city centre at the same time as his friends instead of gazing in shop windows. By the time he'd realised the bus was moving he was too far away to catch it. Chasing after it had been an even bigger mistake: he'd soon blundered off the bus route and into a labyrinth of strange roads from which there seemed to be no escape. He'd passed a paved area with a few benches and a duck pond that he thought he recognised but that was ten minutes ago. Reluctantly he crossed over to the shop.

As he entered Simon caught his shin on an old washstand with a cracked marble top. Presumably this was the quality furniture referred to on the board! The shop itself was one large room, tapering at the back into a tiny alcove. Beyond that was a door, slightly ajar, with frosted glass panels and through these he could see a figure moving. He coughed as loudly as he could without sounding obvious.

"With you in a minute," came a nasal voice from the back room.

Simon decided to browse while he was waiting and found that if the owner of the shop had taken an hour to appear there was more than enough to look at. Around the walls hung framed photographs, paintings and ornamental plates and, despite the size of the room, there was no floor space to speak of. Instead, narrow passages carved their way between piles of tables and sideboards. Stepping into one of these avenues Simon found he was facing a huge gilt mirror with scrolled leaves sprouting around its curved top. Staring back at him was a slightly dust-specked version of himself: average height, average shape, average everything. Considering how unremarkable he looked it was amazing how much time he seemed to spend in front of mirrors. It wasn't vanity so much as an exercise in hope. One day he would walk past a large shop mirror and — *kerpow*! — a new improved face would appear.

He didn't particularly want to be handsome, just noticeable. Even his lunatic friend Matthew had that distinction. For a start, his dark hair spiked naturally in several directions at once whereas Simon's sat obligingly flat on top of his ordinary-shaped head. Then there was his nose. Matthew's nose looked like a prototype for the Channel Tunnel. People took the mickey out of him for it but Simon would willingly have swapped hooters, given the chance. He sneered in disgust at his reflection and moved along to the next avenue where he was confronted by a large stuffed bear, tilted at a precarious angle and with glassy eyes. The thought crossed his mind that it might not be dead, only drunk and looking for a fight. He growled and poked a fist at it.

"Can I help you?"

Simon jumped. Why did he always have to be acting like an imbecile when people caught him unawares? Beside him stood a tall, elderly man, his shoulders stooped. He wore a checked jacket with enormous lapels and an ancient pair of corduroy trousers held up by a thick leather belt. The end dangled down at his side like a wobbly sword. His hair lay in long yellowy waves, streaked with silver and very wiry, and his grey eyes looked remarkably like those of the bear. But the most worrying thing was his nose. Simon could not take his eyes away from it. Maybe I have a thing about noses, he thought. It was a fine specimen and would not have looked out of place on a crow, but protruding a good inch from one nostril was a wodge of what looked like toilet paper.

Simon decided to humour the old man and leave rapidly. "Er . . . sorry." He smiled apologetically. "I was just looking around."

The expression on the man's furrowed face did not change. "Anything in particular you were after?" he said.

"Well, perhaps I could look at your books and things some time but — really I'd just like some directions at the moment."

"Directions?" said the man, looking around. "I don't have a map of the shop, I'm afraid; not like department stores, if that's what you mean."

Was he joking? Simon couldn't tell, but he felt even sillier. "No, I'm trying to get to Nightingale Road swimming baths and I've gone wrong somewhere."

"You could say that." Mr Appleby was definitely smiling now. "It's about two miles away."

"Oh, blimey!"

"Never mind. Come over here." He manoeuvred his way round a stack of old records and pointed out of the side window. "Go down that road, then turn left and you'll find a bus stop. Catch the seventy-eight and ask for Stanley Street. It's only a short walk from there, but you'd best ask again when you get off."

"Thanks — very kind of you." Simon headed quickly for the exit.

"Wait a minute."

Simon stopped. "Er . . . yes?"

"The question is," said Mr Appleby, "do you know how to find your way here again?"

"I'm not sure. Why?"

"Those books and things you wanted to look at."

Trust him to remember that. Simon could see no way out of it. "Oh yes, I think so."

"If you get lost, not saying you will, mind, but if you do just ask for Appy's. Anyone round here will point you right."

"Yes, I'll do that. Thanks."

"You're welcome." And Mr Appy Appleby turned round and walked back into his office as silently as he'd appeared.

Outside in the fresh air, Simon made up his mind to forget his route to the shop as quickly as possible.

Appy had been nicknamed many years before, and like many such names it was the product of sarcasm: his acquaintances had always regarded him as the most miserable devil they knew. It didn't bother him; there were worse names to be called, so he'd been happy to cultivate it. The fact that people thought him eccentric was also no bad thing. It made him quite famous within the neighbourhood, and if mothers pointed him out to their children while staying on the opposite side of the road, why should he worry? Being a 'bogeyman' was a distinction, in its way.

He was less happy that they felt he was mean. Sharing things was all very well, if you had someone to share them with, and he never had — that was all. The answer, as people had occasionally pointed out to him, was marriage, but he'd never been bothered enough, content with his own set pattern of life.

Business had been slow these last few years, though, and he seemed to accumulate more stock than he could sell. Folks peered through the windows, but rarely came in. And as they continued to peer and the shop became more and more cluttered, so a strange rumour had developed.

"Appy's meanness has got the better of him," went the story. "He's gone potty now as well. He's filling up his shop with all sorts of stuff and, do you know, he won't sell so much as a penny whistle to anyone. Why? He's saving it up. Reckons when he dies he's going to take it all with him, wherever he goes!" And they had a good laugh.

Today had seen another addition to the shop, and in unusual circumstances. At half-past nine that morning with no customers in sight, he'd taken time off to relieve himself — a leisurely procedure involving a strong cup of tea to help things along. But while he was placing the mug on the windowsill he had suddenly felt an unpleasantly warm sensation on his upper lip, and cursed. His nose was bleeding, something which seemed to happen with increasing regularity these days. While he was working out how best to stop it, the bell in the inner office rang: a

...ustomer had just come in. The only way to tackle the problem was to grab a piece of toilet paper and plug his nose with that.

"Anyone around?" came a voice from within the shop.

"Hang on, I'm out the back."

And half a minute later he emerged, fairly well patched up, to find a rather scruffily dressed young man, slightly-built and unshaven, with straight, sandy hair, looking out of the side window. He turned round quickly.

"Got something I want to sell," he said. "What'll you give me for this?"

He held up a black case, the length of his arm. Appy took it, placed it on a table and undid the clasps.

"I've had it a few years," the young man ventured, "but it's in good nick."

Appy raised the lid. Nestled into its bed of blue velvet was a saxophone. He lifted it carefully and examined it. He was no expert so far as instruments were concerned, but this one looked to be in good working order.

"I don't know," he said quizzically. "I don't normally take this sort of thing. Musical instruments aren't in my line: no call for them." The man seemed not to be listening but glanced sideways, beyond the shop and into the street. "Well," Appy continued, "I'd be taking it on trust. I don't know if it'll play, or what it sounds like. Unless you care to give me a tune on it," he added.

There was no reaction for a second or two, then the young man looked straight at him and demanded, "Make me an offer, then."

It had to be worth eighty pounds, even if it needed repairing. But Appy was in no mood to be generous. This character's abruptness was annoying him. He would hav said, 'I presume it really is yours to sell?' but somehow h felt he already knew the answer to that.

"All right, I'll give you a tenner for it."

The young man snorted, seemed about to swear, bu finally said, "OK, it's yours. I need the money at the moment Straight cash, though, not a cheque."

"Done." Appy took two five pound notes from an olc tobacco tin in his coat pocket and handed them over. He'c been prepared to go up to twenty-five. The young man tool the notes, shoved them into a trouser pocket and, withou another word, left the shop.

"Shifty bugger," thought Appy. "Still, a business man's got to take a few risks now and then." He replaced the saxophone in its case, and put it on top of a dining chair. "And a bargain's a bargain!"

The swimming lesson was not one of Simon's happiest, for various reasons. The baths had been easy enough to find but half the lesson had gone when he finally appeared at the poolside. He was met by cheers and applause from the rest of his group, and a frosty greeting from Mr Campbell, the games master.

"How long have you lived in this city, Bennett?"

"Fourteen years, sir."

"Really? All your life, eh? A long time — much longer than me, in point of fact. I've only been here a few years."

You snide little toad, thought Simon. Why don't you just get to the point? "Oh, that's interesting, sir. Do you like it here?"

Mr Campbell leaned forward ominously so that his brisk

P.E. teacher's chin was close to Simon's face. "What I'm getting at," he said, "is that if *I* can find my way here so easily, why the hell can't *you*?" His voice had been raised dramatically for the last part of the sentence. Half the people in the pool seemed to be staring at them now including, Simon noticed, a group of girls his own age, dabbling their toes halfway down the other side. Would he look impressive, he wondered, if he picked Mr Campbell up with one hand and deposited him, gurgling, in the deep end?

"Well, Bennett?" He was back to his menacing stage whisper now.

"I missed the bus, sir, and things got a bit out of hand."

Mr Campbell rolled his eyes upwards, as if heaven was somewhere in the spectators' gallery. "Get in the water," he said, and strode away in his smart new trainers.

Bracing himself against the icy waters, Simon curled his toes round the edge of the pool and concentrated all his efforts on not producing one of his famous belly-flops. A hand emerged close to his ankle, grabbed hard, and he toppled forward, smacking the water with his nose and disappearing beneath a column of spray. As he surfaced, spluttering and angry, a cheerful voice close by said, "Wotcha, Si." He syphoned his nose, pushed the hair out of his eyes and found himself facing Matthew Fisher, his lunatic best friend, treading water just out of reach.

"You idiot. You could have killed me."

"Hey that's a point. Tell you what: you climb out and I'll get it right this time."

Simon launched himself at Matthew, missed and nearly drowned again.

"Bennett?"

"Yes, sir?"

"Swim!"

Perhaps it was the presence of the girls, but the only word Simon could conjure up at that moment was breaststroke. So, for a while, he swam slowly and hopefully around them. He might still have been wandering the streets for all the interest they took. He paddled off and spent the rest of the lesson floating on his back, staring at the roof and carefully avoiding the vulture vision of Mr Campbell.

Finally they were whistled out of the pool and herded into the changing rooms, antiquated cubicles with doors that either hung at weird angles, like heads on broken necks, or simply weren't there. Shivering, Simon and Matthew dressed, threw swimming things into sports bags and hared up the steps to the snack bar. Having cornered a table near the viewing window they started to relax. The coffee they'd bought was almost tasteless but welcomingly warm.

"So, what happened to you?" Matthew said. "We thought you'd entered the marathon when you disappeared from view. Expected you to be jogging round the ring road, waving your ears as indicators when you wanted to change lane."

"Ha bloody ha!"

"Where did you get to, anyway?" Matthew was grinning.

Simon could have mentioned the antique shop, but one of the girls had just come into the snack bar, he still hadn't forgiven Matthew for his undignified entry into the water, and it didn't seem particularly important then.

Stuart Bradshaw was living in a dump. According to his rent card it was a basement flat but Stuart knew the truth of the atter: he had been there for over two years now. Water ripped down the kitchen wall, paint flaked in the bathoom and, in the main room, the small window let in barely nough light to see the colour of the carpet. The longer he ad lived there the more he came to resemble the shabbiness f his surroundings. Of course, the drinking didn't help, nor id the more expensive addiction of gambling.

But all that was about to end; good times were just round the corner. Stuart had a plan.

He took the newspaper cutting from the little wooden ox where it had also lived for over two years. The paper ad begun to yellow and tears had formed along the creases. Ie had no need to read it — not for what it would tell him: e knew the details by heart. But the cutting was his lucky alisman, and just at the moment, he needed all the luck he ould get. He read it through religiously from beginning to nd.

Mystery of Student's Disappearance the headline declared. *There is still no trace of black student Calvin Stephens who disappeared two weeks ago. Police say that they have been able to trace the movements of Stephens, a third year Art student at the polytechnic, up to the evening of 7th October when he left a public house in the city centre. Anyone who believes they may have seen him after eight-thirty that evening is asked to contact the police as a matter of urgency.*

Fears were first aroused in a group of fellow students when Stephens did not appear on campus but the search did not begin in earnest until several days later. Stephens is also well-known to jazz-lovers in the city as a talented musician. Friends have apparently expressed their worry that he may have been the victim of a racist attack but police say there is no evidence at this stage to suggest such a theory. Meanwhile they admit there is little they can do until they have more facts at their disposal.

And they could have done, Stuart thought. But I kept my mouth shut all that time. That has to be worth a few thousand of somebody's money. He tucked the cutting into the back pocket of his jeans before leaving the flat and climbing the basement steps to the pavement outside. Just stay calm he said. So long as you keep one step ahead you'll be all right.

Chapter Four

It was five o'clock and already dark when Simon reached home. The air was pleasantly crisp and the last leaves of autumn crackled beneath his feet. As he breathed, the air ahead of him shimmered in the light from the streetlamps and drifted lazily upwards. So long as you had somewhere warm at the end of the journey, walking was one of the best things in the world: hands in pockets, coat collar up, feeling clear-headed and self-contained. He paused before taking out his front door key, savouring the moment.

Inside, the heat of the house was almost overpowering. He threw his coat and scarf over the banisters.

"Hello, dear." His mother appeared at the kitchen door. "Can't you put your coat away in the cloakroom? Your Auntie Vi's coming round this evening and the place looks tidy for once."

The 'cloakroom' was simply the downstairs toilet, in which Simon's father had added a row of pegs running beside the washbasin. It sounded impressive, though, in the same way that they had a patio where most people made do with a back yard. His father had systematically altered the whole house in the ten years they'd been there. He was a fanatical do-it-yourselfer, and every time guests appeared there was always something new for them to admire. Not that his father was available to receive praise; he was too busy hammering and sawing in the garage, clad in his shapeless twenty-year-old working trousers. His latest addition was an extension to the kitchen which would house the new dishwasher. Simon presumed that when he finally ran out of tasks he'd resort to turning the greenhouse into an observatory, or put a crazy-golf course on the roof.

At one time, Simon had been expected to watch and hold paint pots, but he wasn't interested, his dad knew it and the habit thankfully died. Except for family occasions such as meals and visiting relatives, the three of them got along quite happily following their own interests. Simon's interests were many but all concentrated on his room where he could be private, except when his father was putting up new bookshelves. The great advantage was this: if he wanted to go out in the evening the inevitable 'homework' argument started; if he obediently went up to his room and threw his homework under the dressing table no-one knew, no-one bothered him and he was free to concentrate on improving his education in his own way. If music could be heard floating downstairs, his parents assumed he was listening in the same way they did — while he worked. When his mother had finished in the kitchen, Simon made himself a sandwich and a cup of coffee, and retreated upstairs.

His room was permanently untidy. The new bookshelves were already overflowing and little piles had appeared on the floor, on top of the record player and even in the wardrobe. Records lined the base of one wall and an old armchair was covered with clothes. Simon had always been a collector of interesting objects: pieces of driftwood, stamps, coins, cigarette packets — and nothing was thrown away. His mother had once tried to clear some space by disposing of a set of bubble gum cards acquired when he was ten, by much swapping and bargaining. He'd had a minor fit and since then both his parents had left well alone. So long as the stuff *stayed* in his room they felt they'd won a victory of sorts.

The record collection was equally immovable and reflected Simon's listening tastes over the years: pop, folk music, classical and the latest discovery — jazz. He didn't own many jazz records yet, mainly borrowing from the record library until he decided which albums he really wanted. One record, though, was recently bought and, throwing the books from record player to bed, he now placed it carefully on the turntable.

The clothes pile joined the books and he sprawled in the chair. A sinuous music rose from the record player, the swirling staccato notes of an alto saxophone. Charlie Parker, the man they called Bird, soared through *Constellation* and Simon could feel a pressure in his ears and a pent-up desire to shout aloud: the same feeling he'd had on the rollercoaster at last year's fair. Or like the Black ladies at the church his Grandma went to, who jumped up in the middle of a hymn and yelled 'Hallelujah!'

The track finished and Simon could hear his heartbeat in the crackling silence which followed.

The room was solidly furnished: a round rosewood table, Chinese rug and deep velvet curtains gave it the appearance of a furniture showroom for antiques. In the far corner a long-case clock ticked quietly and an open fire burned steadily in the grate, by which the two men sat in deep armchairs. One of the men was smartly dressed and had distinguished greying hair. The other was Stuart Bradshaw.

"Let me get this straight," the smooth man said. "You are asking me for money. A substantial amount of money."

"That's right, Mr Schaeffer."

"I see. And what do I get in return?"

"My silence."

Mr Schaeffer played with the gold identity bracelet on his wrist and adopted a thoughtful expression. "Well, that all seems very simple, but aren't you forgetting something?"

"What?" Stuart wiped a drop of perspiration from above his eyebrow. It must be the fire. He was sitting too close.

"That I already paid you," Mr Schaeffer reminded him. "Two years ago I gave you a very reasonable sum of money for your supposed loyalty. Don't you remember?"

Of course Stuart remembered and this was precisely the kind of teasing conversation he'd expected. Nothing to panic about yet. "I remember," he said. "And I've done what I promised. But I'm short of money and I figured if I just came along and asked you for a handout you'd tell me where to go."

"Too right. So now you're telling me I have to buy your silence in two-year packages. Is that it? Two years from now you'll be back again with your cap in hand and another threatening little speech. Or what happens if you run out of cash a bit earlier? What then, eh?"

"This'll be the only time," Stuart told him.

"Yes. Of course it will be. That's what you'll say next time too. I don't know why I'm wasting my time listening to you. I don't even like having your smelly carcase on my furniture. So let's get to the point shall we? You want money and I don't want to give it to you. My solution's a lot impler. The best way to make sure that you don't go shooting your mouth off to the forces of law and order is for you to disappear. Do you take my meaning?"

This was the moment, though it had come sooner than Stuart had expected. "Fine," he said with as much confidence as he could muster. "I haven't got any family, I haven't really got any friends. I'm a nothing — you don't have to tell me that. But I'm not so stupid that I'd come here and make empty threats. I've got evidence."

He leaned back in his seat and watched for any change in his opponent's expression. But if Mr Schaeffer was surprised he did not show it. "Go on," he said calmly. "So you've got evidence."

"That's right. And if anything happens to me it goes straight to the police."

Had he managed to make that sound as believable as the rest? If he'd known anyone he could trust the plan would have been complete and the statement true. Instead he'd had to improvise and use the Antique Shop for cold storage. But Mr Schaeffer wasn't to know that.

He regarded Stuart quizzically. "Perhaps," he said at last. "It's a bit dramatic but then that's the way you think. You reckon life's a bit like television, don't you?"

Stuart let it pass. He'd made his point: it wasn't up to him to say anything.

"OK. Say I buy it. What are your terms?"

"Do we have a deal then?"

"Depends. You haven't told me just what your evidence is yet. I'm not in the habit of paying for something before I know what it is."

Stuart smiled and found it surprisingly easy to do. "Let's

just say it's the kind of evidence you can't argue against. You show me the cash and I'll show you the evidence."

Mr Schaeffer stood. "Very well," he said stonily.

"Just the two of us."

"Where?"

Spin it out, Stuart thought to himself. Don't be too eager or he'll think he's still in charge. "Oh — I'll phone you," he said. "Say tomorrow evening, or maybe Sunday. We can meet early next week."

Mr Schaeffer showed him to the door. "I hope you know what you're doing," he said as Stuart stepped back out into the cold. He sounded almost like a concerned father. "Because I think you might just be out of your depth here."

"Don't worry, Mr Schaeffer. I can look after myself."

"If you say so, Stuart. If you say so."

The door closed and Stuart took several deep breaths before setting off into the night.

Within the house Mr Schaeffer was already on the phone. The ringing tone stopped and a voice at the other end gruffly answered.

"Jarrod, is that you? Ah good. A little job I'd like doing."

Chapter Five

The following day was grey, windy and very cold. Simon was restless, not wanting to go out, yet feeling cooped up indoors. He whiled away the morning then ran out of ideas. Mr Campbell would have told him to 'show a bit of support for the school' and stand on the sidelines while the Under-15 team were slaughtered at rugby, shouting things like 'Chins up chaps: the game's not lost yet' as the opposing team went thirty points clear. Maybe he would, just for the walk and the look of amazement on old Campbell's face.

"Simon." His mother's voice drifted up to him. He stuck his head out into the landing.

"Yeah?"

"Your dad and I are just going into town. Don't suppose you want to come?"

Well, why not? He didn't exactly fancy the thought of examining appliances for washing-up to see which had the most flashing lights, but he could always wander off somewhere else.

"Just let me get my shoes on."

In the car, as they neared the city centre, he said, "If you like, I'll catch the bus back. Save bother."

His father shrugged. "Fair enough. It's your money."

"Don't forget dinner's at half-past six, though," his mother added.

"Mum, the shops close at half-five. I'll be home in plenty of time for dinner."

His father grunted. His mother contented herself with, "Yes, well we all know you!"

Stuart spent most of the afternoon watching the television. It did nothing to calm his nerves. For one thing, he could not help placing mental bets on all the races and it was typical of his luck that today, when he had no money to go to the betting office, he picked the winners. When his choice for the three-thirty came in at odds of twenty-to-one, he could stand it no longer and left the flat to buy some cigarettes.

Outside the sky was as brooding as his own thoughts. Ever since his trip to see Schaeffer the previous evening he had found himself niggled by small doubts. 'What if?' was the phrase he kept repeating, because you could never predict exactly what would happen, however hard you tried. Even his empty luck on the horses bothered him. It was an omen which he didn't know how to interpret. It might be a good sign of course but equally it could mean that, though his plan was a good one, he didn't have the means to make it work.

Stop it, he told himself. The black case and its contents: they were his salvation. And Schaeffer knew it. He was worried. All Stuart had to plan were the details of the exchange. He rehearsed these in his head and by the time he reached the shops he felt much better. On the way back even the freezing wind failed to lower his renewed spirits; that was, until he was halfway down the basement steps. A knot of panic formed in his stomach halting him in mid-stride. The door was open.

Stuart stared at it, first in disbelief and then horror as he considered what might be waiting for him. He stayed exactly where he was, listening for any sign of movement from inside but the traffic on the road refused to give him the silence he needed. Caution told him simply to turn and run but his feet were acting independently of his brain. He edged closer to the door.

It led into a tiny hallway and Stuart stepped quietly inside, noting as he passed the door that whoever had broken in did not believe in subtlety. The frame had been splintered by a well-aimed boot, the same boot that might still be waiting for him. He stopped again. The sounds of the street were faint enough now for him to concentrate on the main room, though the door to that was firmly closed. There was nothing to hear.

He braced himself and then, with a hoarse yell, he grabbed the handle and flung the door open. It smashed back against the corner of the bed inside, nearly hitting him on the rebound as he dashed in. He swung frantically round waiting for someone to jump — for a sudden rush from any corner of the room. None came. He peered quickly into the kitchen, steadied his breathing, then closed the door and sat on the bed. Only now did the full extent of the damage hit him. Strewn around the room the debris of furniture mingled with small piles of his clothes. The place had been most efficiently turned over.

As he glared at the wreckage, Stuart's anger began to turn into a grim satisfaction. So Mr Schaeffer was playing rough. That was only to be expected. But he hadn't got what he was looking for.

Stuart gathered his clothes together and threw them into

his suitcase: it had been slashed but was still usable. Within ten minutes he had left the flat once more. This time he had no intention of returning.

It didn't take Simon long to exhaust the possibilities of the town. The record shops were packed with people and the few records that looked interesting cost more than he could afford. He perked up when he thought of the library, then remembered it always closed on a Saturday afternoon. It was then that he thought of *Appleby's Antiques*. He couldn't be that far away and there were nearly three hours to kill before dinner. He'd noticed some secondhand books that might be interesting and, come to think of it, there had been a pile of records too. Vastly happier he set off for the ring road to the north of the city centre.

The little pond looked dismal today. Floating cans were more in evidence than ducks, most of whom seemed to be lurking under nearby bushes, out of the bristling wind. Paper bags blew round his feet. On one bench slumped a drunk, half asleep and oblivious of the elements.

Simon decided to find his own way. For one thing there seemed precious few people to ask, and he surely couldn't have forgotten within twenty-four hours. Though it was probably longer than necessary he retraced the exact route he'd followed the day before and, with a little winding back on himself, arrived outside the shop within ten minutes.

Then he stopped. His imagination was taking him for a ride. What was he likely to find in there that could be of any use to him? After all, yesterday he'd stood on this exact spot and vowed never to come here again. On the other hand, why walk all this way for nothing?

He opened the door.

The air inside was barely warmer than in the street, but at least there was no wind. Mr Appleby was removing a picture from the wall. He turned and looked over his shoulder. "Hello," he said. "Didn't expect to see you back so soon."

Simon was relieved to see that the toilet paper had vanished. "No. I just wondered if I could have a look at the books and things."

Mr Appleby climbed down from the chair on which he was standing. "Help yourself. That's what they're there for, though I don't think you'll find any first editions."

"Right. Thanks."

"Fancy a cup of tea?" Appy said, then saw the look on the boy's face: not mistrust so much as confusion. "I don't give drinks to all my customers," he explained, "but it's brass monkeys today and the shop's like an icebox."

Simon smiled. "OK. Yes, I will."

"Good. Go on, you have a look around. I'll be back in a minute or two."

It didn't take Simon long to look through the books. He set aside a paperback of science fiction stories and turned to the records. They were disappointing, the sort that record shops filed under 'Easy Listening' and which he wouldn't be caught dead looking at. He was skimming through the book when Appy returned.

"Here you are. Warm your cockles, this will," he said and thrust a striped mug of strong brew at Simon.

Simon scrutinised the steaming liquid. It looked like thin treacle. "I don't know about my cockles, but it looks strong enough to build my muscles," he said. He felt quite pleased with that. Puns, even weedy ones, were not one of his better known accomplishments.

Appy chuckled. "Not bad," he said. He liked this lad. He was serious in his manner but pleasant with it; the sort people found it easy to make fun of — and Appy knew what that could feel like. "Find anything you want?" he asked.

Simon handed over the book. "I think I'll take this, please. I had a look through the records as well but — "

"Nothing to interest you, hm?"

"Not really. No."

"And what would they be?" Appy enquired.

"Pardon?"

"Your musical interests."

"Oh, jazz mainly. That's what I'm really keen on at the moment."

"I can see why you didn't find much then. I'll show you something you might like to see, though." He moved over to the black case on the dining chair. "Came in only yesterday. Young bloke brought it. Wouldn't have given *him* a cup of tea. Rude bugger. Doesn't hurt anyone to be polite, does it?"

"No." Simon was beginning to see Mr Appleby in a new light. It made quite a pleasant change to meet an adult who called a spade a spade.

"Here, let's take it into the office," he said. "It's warmer in there."

Apart from the fact that there wasn't a bed in the office the effect was remarkably similar to Simon's room. Appy shifted a kettle off a small chair. "Park your bum on there. Now." He unfastened the case. "What do you think of that?"

Words could not describe what Simon thought, nor could

he find anything to say. It was simply the finest thing he'd ever seen and he immediately knew in the pit of his stomach that he wanted it for himself.

"It's . . . fantastic," he managed at last.

"Go on, take it out. Look at it proper."

The saxophone felt both light and heavy at the same time. He wanted to be able to lift it to his lips and blow a flurry of notes that would proclaim: 'I am a musician'. But he wasn't and all he could do was turn it around, gently depress the keys and feel the cold smoothness of the metal.

Appy noted his reaction with pleasure. He pushed the game a little further. "Would you like it?" he asked.

It was like being asked if you wanted to live for ever. Once again, in his head, Simon could hear the frenzy of those winged notes. But why did he want it so much when he knew he couldn't play it? The feeling was stronger than explanations.

"I . . . I could never afford it."

This isn't a game, Appy thought. Not to him. Go on, do the lad a favour. You can afford to. "Well, what would you give me for it?" he said.

"I've no idea. I wouldn't know where to start."

Suddenly Appy made up his mind. "You could have it for ten quid."

Simon's heart missed a beat. He knew it must be worth much more; it certainly was to him. He took the plunge. "Yes. Yes please. I couldn't pay it all now though. Could I give you say two pounds now and the rest in the next couple of weeks?"

"Don't be too hasty. Think about it for a while if you're not sure."

"No. I've made up my mind. Here." He took two pound coins from his pocket. "If you look after it till I've paid you the rest I'll get you the other eight as soon as I can."

Appy placed the saxophone back in its box and smiled at Simon. "Take it now," he said. "I trust you."

The station foyer was a large modern affair, all glass panels and concrete pillars, and the few people in it seemed dwarfs by comparison. Stuart scrutinised their faces but they were all strangers to him. It hadn't taken him long to realise he must have been carefully watched for the break-in to take place with such perfect timing. But watching a flat was one thing: tailing a moving target was a more difficult matter altogether. And he was sly. He had taken several buses on his way to the station, interspersed with circular walks through a maze of different streets.

He slipped the ticket he had just paid for into his wallet and checked the inside pocket of his coat for the padded envelope. This was the beautiful part of the plan: the envelope. Already addressed to his new destination and with the correct stamps licked and in place. It had taken a little ingenuity to calculate the exact weight and bulk of so many fifty pound notes but he had done it.

The phone booth was one of those covered by a plastic dome, making the caller look like a spaceman with a large head. Stuart put in his money and pressed the sequence of numbers. The phone at the other end rang three times before being picked up. No voice spoke. He knows it's me, Stuart thought.

"Afternoon, Mr Schaeffer."

"Stuart. I've been expecting you."

"Which of your apes just turned my flat over?"

"I'll tell Jarrod you appreciated his handiwork, though I don't think he'll be too flattered by your description."

"Jarrod? I might have guessed."

"What do you have to say to me, Stuart?"

"Well, first, it'll cost you a bit more now, what with the damage to my property. Let's say a thousand shall we?"

Mr Schaeffer laughed. It was not pleasant. "You *are* getting bold," he said.

"And I'll take that separately. The rest I want in fifty-pound notes, nice clean flat bundles and we'll call it twenty thousand. That's four hundred notes in case your maths isn't up to scratch."

"And when do you expect me to give you this money, Stuart?"

"Monday morning at half-past ten."

"That's a bit of a tight schedule."

"I don't think so. The banks will have been open long enough by then and, anyhow, you've probably got a damn sight more than that in your own safe. The sort of deals you're involved in you need ready cash, don't you? Your business acquaintances wouldn't be too impressed by a cheque or a gentleman's agreement."

"You're getting decidedly waspish, Stuart. Just because Jarrod demolished your wardrobe without permission?"

Stuart swallowed his anger. "Twenty thousand like I said and I'll see you outside the main post office at ten-thirty. No-one else, please. You can leave Jarrod tethered to his cage. OK?"

"Whatever you say, Stuart. But you still haven't told me what *I'm* getting."

"Use your imagination. You'll get a chance to examine the goods on Monday morning. So long as you're in the right place at the right time."

He replaced the phone on its rest.

The right place at the right time. That was ironic really, considering the fate of the unfortunate Calvin Stephens whose only mistake two years ago had been that he was in the wrong place at the wrong time. Don't dwell on it, Stuart told himself. There are more important things to consider, like where to spend the night. Even a cheap hotel would cost him all that was left of his money, but what did that matter when a couple of days would see him flush again? Thank God he'd got the evidence safely hidden, though. If it had been in the flat and Jarrod had found it, his life wouldn't be worth living.

On his return journey Simon conjured up different ways of smuggling the saxophone into the house. He felt that if his parents knew what he had done they would be scornful at the very least, remembering the piano lessons he'd had when he was younger and the way they'd petered out through his lack of interest and practise. And, if they really wanted, they could be downright obstructive and tell him he wasn't to waste his money on another piece of jumble for people to trip over.

He need not have worried. As he turned the corner of their road he could see that the car was missing. They must still be pressing buttons and having their ears talked off by eager salesmen.

He wasted no time in getting the precious instrument upstairs but then had to find a suitable place to keep it. The case was too large to fit under the bed and too conspicuous anywhere else. Finally, he placed it upright behind an old winter coat at the furthest end of the fitted wardrobe. Humming to himself, he closed the door and strolled downstairs to look at the evening paper which he'd just heard land on the doormat.

Chapter Six

On Sunday afternoon Matthew phoned.

"Do you want to come round and hear the latest composition? I was going to phone yesterday but I thought after the baths you'd probably still not be speaking to me."

Unlike Simon, Matthew was a musician; it ran in the family. His elder sister Carol played the violin, his mother was a flautist and Daniel, two years his junior, was doing very creditably on the cello. Matthew himself was going to be a professional oboist, or a composer, whichever took his fancy. And though Simon would never have told him — Matthew's head was swollen enough already — he wouldn't be surprised if the dream came true. Matthew seemed to be good at most things, usually without trying. His father was the only member of the family who didn't actually play an instrument. By profession, he took flattering photographs of other people's houses for an estate agent. At home he contented himself with the important role of manager, and building up an exhaustive knowledge of musical history.

Simon was in a better mood today. "OK. What's the new masterpiece called?"

"Oh, it hasn't got a title yet. I wanted you to hear it first so you could suggest a few things."

Simon laughed. "You don't need to flatter me."

Matthew seemed genuinely put out. "No, seriously," he

said, "you've got a much better imagination than me. See you about three o'clock?"

"All right. I hope it's not one of your trendy efforts. Like when you played four notes, put the oboe on the floor and meditated over it for five minutes."

"Do you have to remind me about that?" Matthew sounded pained. "That was years ago. I'm not so infantile now."

Simon felt this was the perfect cue to remind Matthew about the attempted drowning but, knowing it wouldn't be appreciated, merely said, "See you at three then."

That was how it was with Matthew. You could never fall out with him for long even if you made a determined effort: he came bouncing back with that usual thick-skinned confidence as if nothing had happened. In that sense they were complete opposites. Matthew was always opening his mouth and promptly inserting his foot; doing the craziest things on impulse and thinking about them later. Simon frequently thought plans through for so long, examining them from every possible angle, that he never got round to doing them.

On reflection he could not really believe that he had committed himself to buying the saxophone the way he had. Not that he regretted it: it was just so out of character. It occurred to him how impressed Matthew would be with his purchase, but apart from the problem of smuggling it out of the house, under the noses of his parents, and back in again, he also knew that once Matthew got his hands on it he would appropriate the instrument to himself. And, as yet, it was still too private for that.

He stuck his head in the garage on the way out.

"See you later, Dad."

"Remember, tea's at half-past five."

Simon shot him a despairing glance. His father raised one eyebrow and the corners of his mouth lifted in a wry smile. "I'm only reminding you because if I don't you know your mum will."

"She already has," he said. "'Bye."

Mr Bennett resumed sawing the leg off an old coffee table.

The Fishers' large semi-detached was only half a mile away. Life there was a hectic, noisy game with everyone trying to monopolise rooms to practise in. By the time Simon arrived, Matthew had managed to corner the front room. He grabbed Simon's arm before he had even had a chance to say hello, let alone take off his coat, and steered him inside. "Sit down over there," he said and had positioned himself at the old, upright piano in the corner before Simon could protest.

"Right," he continued. "It's really for oboe and chamber orchestra but I'll play you the orchestral part on the piano and you can hear the oboe part after. I tried to persuade Carol to play the piano for me but she's gone to the cinema. I told her, one day she'll regret placing entertainment before genius but it didn't make any difference. Anyway, you'll just have to hear it separately for now."

All the Fishers talked a mile a minute and when they stopped, and you thought you could say something at last, they threw notes at you instead. Simon listened patiently to the performance and, even in its present disjointed state, had to admit he liked it more than Matthew's previous offerings. This one at least had a tune he could unscramble.

Matthew finished with a flourish and turned expectantly to him "Well?" he demanded.

"Hm." Simon pretended to debate the matter. "It's all right."

"All right?"

"OK, it's good. I just think your head's big enough already."

Matthew beamed appreciatively. "Thanks. Now your turn. How about a title?"

Simon had forgotten that was his allotted job. He knew he was expected to produce something suitably dramatic. "What about . . . " He pulled a serious face and paused for effect. "*Composition for oboe and orchestra?*"

Matthew threw the sheet music at him.

Stuart was cold. The boarding house where he'd spent the night had strict rules: all bed and breakfast customers to be out by eleven. Since then he'd been on the move again. For a while he had managed to find sanctuary from the weather in an unlocked church but the building had soon begun to feel as cold as the streets outside and even more damp. At the moment he was huddled against the upstairs wall of an unfinished house. He had come across the building site by mistake: the last time he had passed that way was months before and then the site had been occupied by a derelict warehouse. No wonder building contractors managed to make so much money. There were at least twenty cramped little breeze block boxes at various stages of completion. The one he was now in had a roof but no windows, and his feet were turning numb.

It would be tempting to act now, to break this cold

monotony by heading for the shop, but he knew he must be patient. No point in confronting the old man when there was a much simpler way to recover the black case. The shop, after all, had been his other stroke of genius. He had watched it carefully for over a month before putting the plan into action. In all that time he had seen only two customers and they came away empty-handed. The saxophone was as safe there as if he had placed it in a bank vault, and a lot easier to retrieve.

He stood up and stamped his feet on the wooden floorboards in order to restore circulation. Beyond the glassless window night was falling. The shop could only be a short walk away from here, beyond a thin line of grey slate roofs. "Patience is a virtue," he said aloud and pulled his collar up to cover his neck.

Simon looked at the streetlamps that glowed faintly pink outside. "I'd better be going soon," he said.

Mr Fisher's beard appeared round the edge of the door and Simon hastily unspread himself from the full length of the sofa. He swung his feet onto the floor.

"Don't take any notice of me," said Mr Fisher. "Make yourself at home. If we wanted to make our visitors sit upright all the time we'd stick a rod up their back as soon as they came through the front door. Relax."

"Thanks," Simon said, "but I have to leave in a minute."

"Not staying for tea?"

Simon looked at his feet. "Maybe next week."

"We might not invite you next week. Only joking," he added quickly. "By the way, how's your record collection coming along these days?" Mr Fisher's own record collection was two thousand strong and carefully card-indexed.

"All right," Simon told him. "I'm sort of exploring jazz at the moment."

Matthew pulled a face. "Oh dear," he said. "Never mind."

Simon would have liked to thump him for being so smug but Mr Fisher launched his own attack first. "Don't be such a snob," he said. "Jazz is as difficult to play well as classical music so you needn't think of it as being inferior. And it's not something you can simply learn. It's an instinct: you've either got it or you haven't. Try listening to a few great jazz musicians before you start knocking them. You might be surprised by what you hear."

Simon knew what you could hear but until now he hadn't been able to find the words for it. Suddenly he realised why it thrilled him so much. The jazzman spoke through the instrument; the notes were his words, the music his voice. It talked of his fear, excitement, love and anger, and if you listened carefully you could hear and understand. Maybe that was why he most loved the saxophone. It held the man's very breath. Take it away and the man was voiceless, all his feelings trapped within him.

"Anyone in particular?"

Simon hesitated, caught up in his own thoughts. For a moment he hadn't realised he was being spoken to.

"Yes. Charlie Parker."

"Really? I've got a couple of his records if you'd like to borrow them."

Simon couldn't believe his luck. "I'd love to," he said.

Matthew scowled at his father. "I didn't know you had any jazz records," he said lamely.

"Well you don't have to know everything about me. I

hope I'm allowed a few secrets. Anyway, it was the popular music of the day when I was young."

Matthew was out for revenge. "Funny," he said. "I thought you grew up dancing the polka."

Mr Fisher ignored him, speaking instead to Simon. "They're in the back room. Come through and you can take them now."

In the other room he flipped through his box of filing cards, strolled to a long row of records and deftly removed two from the middle. He handed them to Simon. "One of them's a live recording," he said. "The sound's a bit ropy but you really get a sense of atmosphere." He paused. "Pity the Umbrella's not open these days," he said.

Simon was baffled by his sudden change of tack. What did umbrellas have to do with making music? Mr Fisher caught his expression. "Sorry. Thinking aloud," he said. "The Umbrella Club was the best place in this part of the world for jazz. Better than London some people said, though I wouldn't know about that. Closed a couple of years ago though."

"Why?" Simon asked.

"Their star performer disappeared."

"Disappeared?"

"Just that. Young Black musician. Simply vanished. I wish I could remember his name: it was quite unusual as I recall. Stephen something I think."

"Very unusual!" Matthew observed sarcastically.

"I wonder if Joan remembers," said Mr Fisher unperturbed. "She has a better memory for names than I do."

He called to his wife but she was upstairs and otherwise occupied. "Never mind. It'll probably come back to me

later," he said. "Hope you enjoy the records." And he saw
Simon to the front door.

The air outside was colder than Simon had expected. He
walked briskly home under a sky already black with night.

Appy lived over the shop. Though the upstairs contained
household amenities of bedroom, bathroom, living room
and kitchen, it was in all other respects an extension of the
shop: a gallery of his favourite acquisitions. The wall-space
was covered with a wide variety of paintings, and many
people would have been surprised at their quality: Appy
had an eye for a work of art and did not place store on
flashy, and often fraudulent, signatures. Real art stood out
from its imitators like snow on the coalhouse roof.

Over the bed where Appy now lay hung a German
Madonna and Child from the sixteenth century. The
painting would have graced any public gallery and , indeed,
at least one had made him a sizeable offer after he'd shown
it to their experts for advice. But he would never part with it.
He'd had it so long it was like a piece of him, and somehow
it was a comforting picture too. He wasn't a particularly
religious man but there was something safe in the mother
with her young son cradled carefully in her arms; and
peaceful. Maybe the painter had left some of *his* belief in the
paint before he died. Who could tell?

Appy was sliding gently into sleep when he heard the
noise. He knew immediately what it was. The bedroom was
over the front of the shop and the muffled splintering sound
that rose through the floor came from the front door.
Someone was breaking in.

He stayed where he was, ears strained to catch any

movement from below. His real fear was if they should come upstairs. So long as they stayed in the shop they could take whatever they wanted. Phoning for help was out of the question as the only telephone was in the office. He'd just have to wait until they left — if they left.

Quietly removing his dressing gown from the bedside chair Appy climbed cautiously from the bed and padded to the head of the stairs. There was no discernible noise now, a good sign in a way. If they wanted to avoid disturbing him, maybe they also wanted to leave him alone.

He waited for five minutes, tensed for any footstep on the stairs. None came and the shop seemed as silent as the night air. He could stand the strain no longer. If it was a trap he was walking into he'd rather face it than stand there another moment. Avoiding the treads he knew would creak, he crept downstairs.

The shop was completely dark except for a single shaft of light from a lamp on the street corner. This shone directly through a gap in the shop door — now hanging open. Appy knew the vast stacks of furniture could conceal anyone, any number of intruders who might be there. He pressed the main light switch, not caring now so long as he could see them rather than keep them crouching in the recesses of his imagination.

Lights flooded everything. Appy blinked, then gritted his teeth and tentatively began to examine every row and gap in the place. As he proceeded his fear gradually diminished. Not only was no-one there; there was no sign of anything missing. Nothing seemed even to have been moved.

But someone had been there. The door to the office was ajar so they'd looked in there and, as he stood by the front oor, the cold stinging his cheeks, he could see how cleanly nd expertly the lock had been smashed.

tuart blundered along the streets near the shop. It could ot be true: the impossible had happened and the instrunent had gone. Unless — he stopped suddenly. Of course, he old man must have taken it upstairs. In his initial panic uch a simple fact had failed to cross his mind. He would ave to go back.

He turned — and immediately saw the car. Lit only by its idelights, Stuart realised straight away: he didn't need to ee the faces inside. As he watched, the headlights were urned full on and the vehicle accelerated towards him. The vhiteness stabbed his eyes as he swung back round and fled lown the street. Near the end was an alleyway between two iouses. He bolted down it, his feet slapping against the tone slabs, and emerged in a small back garden. From the iouse came a shrill barking, quickly drowned by the screech of the car's wheels on the road outside.

The only way was forwards. He careered down the iarrow path, across a vegetable patch and over the wall it the bottom. He was standing in a mirror image of the garden he had just left. All the property round here was back to back'. That meant, if he was lucky, there would be an identical alleyway too. He headed towards the iouse, negotiated a low wooden gate at the top of the lawn and, sure enough, there facing him was the passageway.

Once in the road beyond, Stuart stopped again and listened. No footsteps. No car. But it would only be a matter of time. Then he realised: the street had a familiar look to it, and not just because it was built on a similar plan to the one he had left. Something about the pattern of the roofs or the design of the front doors. He had walked down it earlier in the evening on his way from the building site to the shop. Stuart needed somewhere to run and, just at that moment, the building site seemed the only place in the world. Half running, half gasping, it took him five minutes to get there.

Installed in his makeshift watchtower he scanned the waste-ground around him. There was no sign of the car and as the minutes ticked by he relaxed slightly. He took a packet of cigarettes out of his coat pocket, lit one then turned back to the window. Still nothing. He blessed his luck: if there hadn't been that alleyway to delay their progress he'd have stood no chance.

"Stuart?" The voice echoed sibilantly in the empty structure of the house. It came from directly underneath. Did they know he was here? They couldn't; they were only bluffing. But what if they'd heard him strike the match?

Then, the footsteps on the exposed wood of the stairs. They were in no hurry. They knew.

A head appeared at floor level.

"Ah, there you are, Stuart. You are a silly boy. Why waste your energy?"

In fear and hatred he rushed to the top of the stairs and swung wildly with his foot. A hand caught his flailing leg easily and threw him off balance. He fell heavily on his back, winding himself badly. When he looked up both men were over him. He scuttled crab-like to the wall.

Within seconds they had hauled him to his feet and forced

one arm up behind his back so his wrist dug into his shoulder blade. He winced and nearly fell again. Mr Schaeffer spoke quietly into Stuart's face.

"This is what you call the day of reckoning, Stuart," he said. "You know, you're not such a slippery customer as you think. We've been watching you since Friday night — in fact Jarrod isn't so slow after all, are you Jarrod? Did I mention, Jarrod, that Stuart here reckons you're an ape?"

Jarrod smiled in chilling acknowledgement.

"But as for you coming back here — well, we never thought you'd be as daft as that."

"What are you going to do?" Stuart managed through the pain.

"Ask you a few questions for a start. Like 'Where is it?'"

"I don't know. It's not in the shop so your guess is as good as mine."

"Exactly. So you're not a lot of use any more, are you?"

"Hang on a minute."

"Well?"

"You don't know what you're looking for yet."

"Oh, don't I?" Mr Schaeffer leaned closer to Stuart, so their faces were nearly touching. "How about a black case containing a saxophone?"

"Fine. So go and find it."

Jarrod reached over from behind Stuart's back and violently twisted his jaw. Mr Schaeffer smiled appreciatively. "Have I forgotten something?" he said. "Because if I have you'd better tell me. I might even decide to show a bit of mercy. You never know."

Stuart knew only too well. A word like mercy only passed Mr Schaeffer's lips for the purpose of mockery. Stuart was filled with hatred and fear. "Something small," he grated. "But very incriminating."

"That'll do," Mr Schaeffer said equably and turned to gaze abstractedly out of the window.

Stuart struggled, but Jarrod's hold on his head had tightened to a vice-like grip. He was thrust to the rough wooden floor and felt the sudden pressure of a knee in his back. Jarrod was waiting for instructions. The man at the window turned sideways and gently inclined his head.

It took both men to lift the body and drop it from the open window, headlong, onto the pile of bricks beneath.

Back in the car the two men looked at each other.

"Why'd you search his pockets?" Jarrod said.

Mr Schaeffer waved a wallet and a large folded envelope at him. "Point one," he said chirpily. "Make it difficult to identify him. No reason to make life easier for the forces of law and order. And besides — " He shrugged.

"Besides, what?"

"Oh, just curious."

They drove off into the anonymous night.

"I suppose we shall just have to visit the junk shop," said Mr Schaeffer.

Chapter Seven

That night Simon slept badly. All he could remember next morning was the general feeling of anxiety that had pervaded his dreams, and one detail: a cramped space that was black above his head and black beneath his feet, in which he was helplessly pinned, like a butterfly that was not quite dead. Everything else had vanished with the arrival of daylight.

He was up before his parents and, as he was unlikely to be interrupted for a while yet, he took the black case from the wardrobe and sat down on the end of his bed to examine the saxophone again. The metal was tarnished, but in all other respects the instrument seemed perfect. He wished again that he could play it, but knew there was no point in trying. It lay mute in his hands.

He was almost content just to look at it, though; to admire the workmanship that had produced it. He ran his fingers over the ornate pattern carved round the name on the bell of the instrument — a wonderful arabesque of lines like copperplate handwriting that had grown foliage. 'Selmer', it proudly proclaimed.

As his eyes followed the weaving design, he noticed some smaller letters contained within it. They were burnished in just as beautifully in a similar style, but they looked somehow fresher. He tilted the saxophone against the light in order to see them more clearly. 'c.s.' he read. Was that the maker's trade mark, or did it refer to something else?

67

There was a noise on the landing. Hastily replacing the instrument and its case in the wardrobe, Simon went down stairs. He wanted to be first down today, to set the breakfast table. It always helped if you wanted to ask a favour.

At breakfast he waited until his father was on his second cup of coffee before he dropped the question. Upstairs holding the saxophone, he had suddenly realised that it was not really his yet. And he wanted to remedy that as soon as possible.

"Dad, d'you think I could have an advance on my pocket money?"

His father surveyed him over the newspaper. "I knew there had to be a reason," he said. Simon looked blankly innocent. "Anything special you want it for?"

"Sort of, but I can't really explain at the moment." He knew it was a feeble answer but it would have sounded even more stupid to say 'No'. Fortunately his father seemed in a generous mood.

"How much?" he said.

"Oh, thanks Dad."

"I haven't given it to you yet."

"Sorry. Eight pounds please." He felt it might be a little risky asking for it all at once but it would save asking again. The worst his father could do was refuse.

His father reached into his jacket, which was hanging over the back of the chair. "You're lucky I went to the bank on Friday," he said, as he handed over a five pound note and three coins. "When will you let us in on the secret?"

"Soon," Simon said, carefully avoiding the suspicious gaze of his mother.

*   *   *

68

The grey car was parked just up the road from *Appleby's Antiques*. From where they sat the two men had a clear view of the entrance to the shop. They had been there since half-past eight; past them the last straggling children had made their way to school. Now, three-quarters of an hour later, the street was still again. There was no sign of activity from the shop.

At nine twenty-five, Appy moved the table that had been acting as a temporary barricade from behind the front door. The police had come and scrutinised the door, dusted for fingerprints and left, shaking their heads pessimistically. But no locksmith had been available on the Sunday, so he'd had to do the best he could. He'd only just managed to get hold of someone to make the repairs, having phoned on and off for the last twenty minutes. They didn't seem too eager for custom. Appy reasoned that, as burglaries seemed always to be on the increase, maybe locksmiths had more custom than they needed. He wished he could say the same of the secondhand furniture business.

Today, however, trade arrived earlier than expected. He'd hardly replaced the table in its proper slot when the door opened and two smartly dressed men entered. One was in his forties, his sleek hair greying; the other a younger man, probably in his mid-thirties. Both were heavily built. To Appy they looked rather out of place in their clothes, like furniture removers called suddenly to a funeral. The elder one sported a camel-hair coat.

Appy approached them. "Morning. Can I help you at all?"

The older man gestured expansively with his right hand, encompassing everything in the shop. "Just looking," he explained.

"Help yourself," said Appy and perched, out of the way on the arm of a chair near the office.

The two men strolled round. As he watched them, Appy felt they were not so much examining the goods he had to sell, as searching for a particular item. After a couple of minutes the older man approached him. "I may as well be blunt," he said. "I was given to believe that you might have something belonging to me."

Appy stood up. "Oh, yes? And what might that be?"

"Well, my nephew told me he brought it in the other day — a saxophone in a black case. Unfortunately, it wasn't exactly his property. I don't want to go into all the personal details, but I'm afraid he was in a bit of financial difficulty. Last week he paid me a visit and approached me for money; I refused. He's borrowed before and he tends to be rather, shall we say, unreliable. It wasn't till later that my son discovered his saxophone was missing. I'm afraid my nephew had decided to take matters into his own hands."

He paused, obviously waiting for some response. Appy shrugged. "Yes, he brought it in last Friday, but I'm afraid it's gone now. Quick sale."

The two men exchanged glances. "I see," said the older one. "That makes things a bit tricky, doesn't it? I realise it wasn't your intention, but you did in fact receive stolen property."

Appy knew he was on delicate ground. Remembering the young man who'd sold it to him, he wasn't altogether surprised. But he did not like the implied threat.

"And, of course," the man continued, "it means whoever bought it from you is in a rather awkward spot too." He suddenly smiled. The smile had a slightly sickly edge to it. "I hink the easiest thing for everyone is if I contact the purchaser: you do keep records don't you? I'll reimburse you for the loss, of course. Genuine mistake. Not your fault."

He removed his wallet and Appy could see an array of ten pound notes. This man seemed used to paying for things, and, judging from his attitude, to getting what he wanted. Appy had no desire to fall foul of the law but he did not like, or trust, the arrogant man who thrust a handful of notes towards him.

"As it happens, I don't record names and addresses unless people pay by cheque. This was cash."

The man paused. "I see." His smile vanished.

"Of course," Appy added. "I don't want you to be out of pocket either." He took the tobacco tin of money from his own pocket and removed the lid. "What would you say it was valued at? On your insurance, I mean."

There was an icy silence between the two men. Camel-hair carefully closed the wallet and replaced it in an inside pocket.

"It is important to me," he said. "I really would appreciate your co-operation. Perhaps you could tell me what the buyer looked like."

"Not really." Appy was evasive. "I had quite a few customers on Saturday. Difficult to remember faces."

"Perhaps it will occur to you later. It would be very helpful if you could remember. We'll keep in touch."

Appy said nothing. The two men left the shop unhurriedly, leaving the door wide open behind them. Appy shivered. Maybe he should have mentioned the boy. But he knew that even if the story of the saxophone's theft were true, which he seriously doubted, the instrument meant more to that boy than it ever would to Camel-hair. If the worst came to the worst it could always be sorted out when he came back with his money.

He met Matthew as they were filing into registration and thumped him cheerfully on the arm. Matthew evinced great pain and clutched the wounded limb. "I'll never play the violin again," he said dramatically.

"Oboe," Simon corrected him.

"Oboe. Ah, yes." Matthew rapidly recovered. "Oh by the way, I've got a message for you."

"Oh yes?"

"Nothing exciting," he said, and kicked his bag under the desk.

"Well, don't keep me in suspense."

Matthew yawned. "Earth-shattering piece of information from my father, that's all."

"Oh." Simon tried to keep the disappointment out of his voice.

"Quite," Matthew continued. "Anyway, I'd better deliver it or he'll be harping on at me all week. It's that jazz musician he was on about, the one whose name he'd forgotten. Well, he and my mum worked it out between them. It wasn't Stephen anything. He was called Calvin Stephens.

It was a weird sensation. The saxophone, until that morning an anonymous musical instrument, had suddenly become something personal; even stranger that he knew who must have owned it, yet remained completely unaware of the man himself. What had he looked like? How old was he? Young, Mr Fisher had said. A young Black musician. At several points during the day Simon found himself trying to visualise the saxophone in the hands of its original owner, pouring music into the smoky air of a crowded club.

School finished at half-past three, so it was not until ten past four that he reached the shop. The lights were on. Simon pushed the door handle, eager to get the transaction completed, but the door remained stubbornly closed.

Oh no, he thought. Surely he's not closed early today. Just then Mr Appleby's head appeared behind the glass.

"Just give it a good shove," he called.

Simon tried again and this time the door opened suddenly, propelling him into the shop faster than he'd intended. Mr Appleby looked peeved. "Bloody locksmith," he said. "Takes half a day to get here then makes a dog's breakfast of the job."

Simon closed the door firmly. From inside the shop the new lock was only too obvious. "What happened?"

"Not a lot. Someone broke in on Saturday night, then left empty-handed."

Simon looked puzzled, then concerned "Are *you* all right?"

"Bless you." Appy smiled. "That's a kind thought. Yes, I'm fine. They'd gone when I came downstairs. Probably took one look at all this old rubbish and decide they'd better try somewhere else. Anyhow, if they'd tried shifting any of it they'd quite likely have given themselves a hernia. Most of this stuff hasn't been moved for years." He ushered Simon into the back office. "Brought your money already?"

"Maybe."

For a moment Appy thought he'd come to say he couldn't afford it after all, then Simon produced the money with a triumphant flourish.

"Here you are. I managed to get all eight."

Appy looked impressed. "Means a lot to you, that old saxophone, doesn't it?"

Simon nodded.

"Have you tried it out yet?"

"Well actually . . . " Simon didn't know how to explain.

"I understand. You can't play it, can you?"

"How did you know?"

"I watched you when you first picked it up. I could tell it was really special to you, but any musician would have tried it out before he bought it. You turned it round like it was a piece of sculpture. And why not? I suppose it is in a way."

Simon looked rueful. "I feel a bit of a fraud, really."

"No need to." Appy put his hand on Simon's shoulder. "Things aren't special because they're useful." He turned and moved briskly out of the office to the stairs at the back of the shop. "Stay here a minute. I just want to fetch something to show you."

He was gone less than a minute. When he returned he was carrying two identical tins. He placed them on the desk.

"See these? There's a story behind them."

He opened the first one. It was split into two compartments. "These were dished out to soldiers in the First World War," he said. "That side had cigarettes, this side chocolate. It was a sort of morale-booster."

He could see Simon looked puzzled, so he opened the second tin. Simon gasped, then grinned at him.

"They're all there. All the cigarettes and the chocolate too. Some poor bugger never got round to using them."

Appy sat down on the arm of Simon's chair. "Now, why should I want to keep that old tin? It doesn't serve a purpose. But I can tell from how you looked when I opened the lid that you understand.

"I don't know if even I can explain why that tin's special to me, but I think it's because it belonged to someone once. I imagine what he might have looked like and what he was thinking when his time came. It's not just things, you see; it's the people."

Simon felt a great affection for this unusual man. He would have liked to hug him, but was afraid to; he stood up and held out his hand. Appy looked surprised for a moment, then shook it warmly.

"Goodbye, Mr Appleby. You've been very kind."

How many people had ever said that to him? He beamed and looked a little sheepish. "Yes, well maybe we'll see you again when you've got a moment."

"Yes, I hope so. Er . . . 'bye for now."

Simon picked his way through the shop, remembered to pull the door hard and waved back through the window. He set off cheerfully down the street.

Out of the shadows slid a grey car, like a shark scenting blood.

Chapter Eight

As Simon walked towards the city centre the car cruised slowly behind, at a steady distance. In this manner it followed him for several minutes, stopping when necessary, biding time. When it finally gathered speed and drew alongside him at a set of traffic lights he was entirely unaware of its presence, or of the well-dressed man in the passenger seat who now observed him. Nor could he guess that the school uniform he wore, and which was illumined by the neon glare of a shop window, was being meticulously noted.

The lights changed and Simon crossed the road. In due course the car also moved on its way, gliding anonymously into the flow of rush-hour traffic.

It had been a long day. Simon felt exhilarated but tired, and after tea he settled down in front of the television, quite happy to watch and relax. At half-past nine he was already falling asleep. He yawned loudly and, declining the offer of a milky drink, left his parents downstairs. He did not even look at the instrument which now belonged unquestionably to him; he had barely enough energy to climb under the covers.

Sleep overtook him rapidly and he tumbled gratefully into its depths. It was not long, however, before he was forced to visit that same darkness which had held him a prisoner the night before. The more he tried to escape from its depths, the more firmly he seemed thrust into it. Exerting himself to the point where he thought his lungs would collapse and his bones crack and fall apart, he spun suddenly free, and drifted weightlessly into an area of calm.

The morning dawned clear and promising. As Simon drew back the curtains he saw the first hint of sun for nearly a week: a pale luminosity that infused the air outside. He dressed swiftly and was tying his shoelaces when there was a sudden heavy thud from within the wardrobe. His mother's voice called.

"What was that, Simon?"

"Nothing, Mum. Just knocked a pile of books over. Sorry."

"I'm surprised there's any room for them to fall," she teased, and Simon could hear her footsteps moving down the stairs.

He slid open the wardrobe door and found the black case lying awkwardly across a pair of slippers, its fastenings undone by the force of the impact. Opening the lid, he carefully removed the saxophone before hauling the case on to the floor. As he did so, he noticed that the case had suffered from the fall. The velvet base inside, so carefully shaped to take the curves of the instrument, had come adrift. It had seemed solid, but was rather like the moulded tray in a chocolate box which could be removed, usually to reveal another layer beneath. He adjusted it so that it would fall back into place, but something seemed jammed and it remained projecting awkwardly at one end. He would have to remove it completely and start again.

He tipped the case so that the padded lining fell to the floor; there was a clatter, and something else fell too. It was a small plastic box that must have been lying at the bottom of the case. He picked it up. Through its clear plastic he could see that it contained a tape cassette. He took out the tape and turned it over but there were no markings to indicate what it might contain.

"Breakfast," his mother called.

There was no time to find out now. Curious, he placed the tape with a small pile of similar boxes on his dressing table, tied his remaining shoelace and ran downstairs.

Apart from a small but painful encounter with Mr Campbell in the gym, the day at school was uneventful. Mr Campbell was one of those teachers who could not stand to have his authority challenged, and that included pupils failing to arrive on time for his lessons.

Simon and Matthew had spent their breaktime keeping warm in the library and had consequently been awarded the tedious job of shelving books by the librarian. The library was the worst place in the school for hearing the bell. Everyone knew that. They pointed all this out to Mr Campbell while the others in the class sat ready and eager in their P.E. kits. Of course, it made no difference. Mr Campbell was not susceptible to reason at the best of times and Simon's face was already fixed firmly in his mind on account of the swimming baths episode.

"Don't bleat at me," he snapped. "You're late and that's all there is to it."

"Why don't you ask the librarian?" Matthew suggested. "Mrs Montague."

"I know who she is, thank you."

"Well, she'll tell you. It wasn't our fault."

Mr Campbell turned on Simon. "And what about you? Do you want to make life more difficult for yourself as well? Go on, let's hear your excuse."

"Same as his," Simon said. "Only it's not an excuse."

"Right. Well we know what happens now, don't we?"

Simon and Matthew exchanged looks.

"Don't we!"

"Yes, sir."

"And is there any reason I shouldn't?"

Simon knew he should keep his mouth shut but he was fed up with this bombastic man in his purple tracksuit who favoured the thugs and bullied the rest. "Yes," he said and took a deep breath.

"Go on," Mr Campbell said menacingly.

"No-one's allowed to use corporal punishment in this school except the Head and his deputy — and then they have to get our parents' permission." Matthew stared at him in amazement and Mr Campbell's fingers twitched.

"Is that right?" he sneered.

Matthew leapt in with a show of solidarity. "That's right," he said. "You're out of order."

The rest of the class waited expectantly. They knew full well that once the changing room door was closed on the world outside, school rules no longer applied. Mr Campbell was master of his own kingdom.

"I think you'd better come into my office," he said softly. And there he had administered his plimsoll punishment. The strange thing was that Simon and Matthew did not feel humiliated. Rather it was a shared experience that reinforced the bonds of their friendship. In fact, by the end of the day, when the stinging sensation had worn off, they were feeling quite pleased with themselves.

By half-past three the car was parked close to the school gates. Its occupants were waiting, like anglers over a single rod; their eyes never left the pavement just beyond the gate. As they watched they talked, never turning their heads but directing each word at the windscreen in front of them. The driver spoke first.

"We could still be on a hiding to nothing. How do we know this kid's got anything to do with it?"

"We don't," Mr Schaeffer replied, smoothing back the greying hair at his temples. "But then again, we don't know he hasn't. At the moment he's the only lead we've got. The old man's had no other customers since we started watching. That makes the boy worth checking out."

"OK. If you say so."

"I say so."

The driver lapsed again into silence.

"And I've got a feeling that wasn't the first time he'd paid the old man a visit. They were too chummy."

At that moment a group of boys and their girlfriends came shoving and joking out of the school gates. The two men intensified their vigil. A few minutes later two boys emerged, chatting together.

"That's him." Mr Schaeffer opened the car door. "I'll be back in a while."

He strode purposefully towards the boys and spoke to the taller of them. "Excuse me," he said.

Simon stopped and looked at him uncertainly.

"You don't know me," the man began, "but I have a message for you. At least I think it's for you. I hope I've got the right person. What's your name?"

"Simon Bennett." It was an instinctive reply. Years of answering teachers had seen to that.

"Ah, good. I am right then. It's from Mr Appleby."

Simon relaxed slightly. "What did he want to tell me?"

"Well, it's about the saxophone you bought." He watched the boy's face. If he didn't have it they were back to square one. He was prepared for a look of blank incomprehension, but instead the boy seemed concerned.

"What about it?" Simon was annoyed. Why had Appy told this stranger about their deal? It was a private affair between the two of them. He tensed imperceptibly.

"He says there's something needs fixing on it and, of course, he wants you to get the best out of it. Says he'd like you to take it back for a while — so he can get it repaired."

Simon was on his guard now. "Who are you?" he demanded.

"Just a business acquaintance," the man said. "I was passing this way so I said I'd let you know. Anyway, if you drop it in to him as soon as you can, he'll do the rest."

Simon had no intention of doing any such thing. Appy knew he couldn't play the instrument, so this man's story had to be untrue. But how did he know about the saxophone in the first place? He stared hard at the stranger, stony-faced, and tried to keep the truth out of his voice.

"Yes," he said. "I'll do that."

Matthew had been staring politely in the other direction. Simon turned and tugged his sleeve. "Thank you for telling me," he called back as they walked away.

Mr Schaeffer stood for a moment, then headed back to the car. The boy was smart. Whatever he might have promised to do, he had not swallowed the story. But at least they now knew his name and maybe the old man could help them out, with a little persuasion.

Matthew may have kept at a discreet distance but he also had good hearing. As they walked to the bus stop he was full of questions: What was that all about? Saxophone? What saxophone? Simon promised him a chance to see the instrument soon and, if he wanted, to try it out. But about the strange meeting, and what it might signify, he said nothing. It wasn't that he didn't trust Matthew, just that he was not yet ready to confide.

Simon was still brooding when, twenty minutes later, he approached his house. Now was probably the time to seek his parents' advice, but he shied away from complicated explanations. As well as criticising him for buying the instrument in the first place, he felt sure they would treat him to one of those childhood speeches he remembered so well, the one that began: 'How many times have I told you not to talk to strange men?' They might also tell him to keep away from *Appleby's Antiques*, and that was one thing he must carefully avoid. For he realised that the only way to find out what was going on was to consult Appy himself.

As he reached the end of his drive, the paperboy skidded past on his bike. "Here you are," he said. "Save me riding all over your lawn." And he was gone again.

Simon tucked the paper under his arm in order to cope with both schoolbag and front door key. Once inside, he dropped his bag and took the paper through to the living

82

room: his mother would be in soon and always expected the first read. The headline was a large one:

BODY FOUND ON BUILDING SITE

Without taking off his coat Simon read the rest of the article. It began in the dramatic style beloved of all journalists:

> *Yesterday morning workmen on a city building site discovered more than they had bargained for when they examined what they had originally believed to be a bundle of clothes.* There followed a talkative eye-witness account from two of the workmen, then: *Police have not yet released the name of the dead man but say there is no suggestion at this stage of foul play. A police spokesman said, "We merely wish to ascertain the man's movements up to the time of his death. In particular, we should like to hear from anyone who may have been in the area where the incident occurred some time between Sunday evening and the early hours of Monday morning."*

The paper then drew its own moral about the dangers of open building sites, reminding parents to warn their children and to make sure they knew what they were doing after dark. Simon smiled grimly. He had no doubt that, after she'd read the article, his mother would do precisely that.

Simon folded up the account of police investigations and other serious news, and placed the paper on the dining table where his mother would quickly find it. Then he remembered something else that needed to be investigated. He had time before tea to hear what, if anything, was on the recently discovered tape. He threw his coat over the banister and ran upstairs.

His tape recorder was a small, portable affair combined with a radio, that he used mostly when the family went on holiday. It was not exactly good quality but would do for now. The cassette was already re-wound to the beginning of side A, so he simply loaded it and pressed the start button. There was an extended empty hissing and, for a while, he thought it must be a blank tape. Then came a sudden click and the sound of applause fading out. Immediately a small jazz group burst into an up-tempo number. The pace was furious, powered along by the sax player. The other musicians seemed to be fighting to stay with him. But it wasn't the speed alone that mesmerised Simon: every note was clear and precise, every phrase perfectly constructed, soaring out of the one before in a seemingly endless flow of imagination.

The applause as the soloist finished was ecstatic. The audience were swept along in the same way as the musicians. There followed a competent piano solo and one on the bass which was almost impossible to hear properly, however much Simon fiddled with the tone controls. Finally the saxophone re-emerged, driving the piece to a thunderous close.

Simon knew who had to be playing, but part of him still felt it was impossible. He thought again of the tiny carved initials and understood what that saxophone must have meant to Calvin Stephens, who had played it with his soul and left his mark lovingly on its golden surface.

The applause died down and the next number began, a

slow haunting ballad. Simon fetched the instrument and placed it on the bed. Kneeling on the floor he rested his face on his hands, inches from the open bell. It was a strange sensation to hear this passionate music and to stare at the dark cavern from which it had poured.

The track finished and, halfway through the applause, there was another click and the hissing returned. He listened until the end, but the rest was blank. He switched off the cassette recorder and cradled the saxophone in his arms. It was as if, by holding the instrument and listening to the sound it made, he had begun to know the man himself.

Chapter Nine

Day emerged from night, imperceptibly and without dawn. The sun remained hidden firmly behind a solid white fog that rose from the damp ground, smothering every house and shop in the city. For a while, the air glowed orange around the still-lit streetlamps, but soon even that colour vanished leaving a world bleached, heavy and opaque.

Appy woke cold. He inhaled and his lungs burned softly; his fingers cracked and all the bones in his body shuddered in sympathy. Why did winter make him old, he wondered as he fished in an overcoat pocket for his fingerless shop-keeper's mittens. He wrapped his numb hands round a mug of hot tea, and his fingertips tingled.

The shop was freezing. As he shuffled to the door the furniture, stacked in soldierly ranks, smelled musty. He turned the key, slipped the bolt and peered out. The road was barely visible beyond the pavement's edge. Leaving the door closed, as if to keep the fog at bay, he turned towards his office. He had taken four paces when the door opened. Out of the fog stepped a man.

Appy recognised him immediately. The camel-hair coat was now complemented by a pair of suede gloves and a blue silk scarf. In all other respects nothing had changed.

"Good morning, Mr Appleby." The man removed his gloves and rubbed his hands vigorously together. "If that doesn't seem an inappropriate greeting. Devil of a day isn't it?" He cast a glance out, beyond the pane of glass, then closed the door.

Appy was not inclined to waste time in idle conversation. This man made his hackles rise; the sooner he left, the better. "What can I do for you?" he asked briskly.

"A promising start, Mr Appleby. I'd be most obliged of your assistance, I can tell you. Perhaps we could make ourselves a little more comfortable while we discuss the matter." He looked hopefully towards the back of the shop. Appy took down a dining chair and thrust it towards him.

"Very well." He smiled. "I'm sure we can manage equally well here." Flicking the chair with his gloves, he positioned himself so that he remained half-standing and continued. "I know who you sold the saxophone to."

Appy could not disguise his surprise. "How?" he asked, before he had time to think.

"Not with so much difficulty as you might suppose. However," — he brushed the question aside as he had the dust on the chair— "that's immaterial to the matter in hand, which is . . . " He leaned forwards and fixed Appy with his piercing grey eyes. "The recovery of the instrument."

Appy returned his stare. "If you've found the buyer, what's your problem?"

"The buyer is the problem: a most tenacious young man. I think he must be rather attached to his purchase. Now, I don't really want to make life difficult for him; he presumably doesn't realise the seriousness of his position. So I felt the best thing would be a friendly word from someone he knows."

Appy's eyebrows lifted slightly. "Meaning me?"

"Precisely. I felt sure you'd understand."

What entitled him to be so sure of everything? Again Appy felt the overwhelming urge to hinder him, to thwart his well-laid plans. He thrust his hands into his pockets. "And how am I supposed to do that? He's paid his money, he's not likely to come back and I told you before I don't know his address."

"Ah, but I know where to find him. If you'd be so good as to write a brief note explaining the situation, it would be no problem to deliver it."

Appy had heard enough. He stared at the dispassionate face of the man leaning on his chair and said quietly, "I think you should call the police."

"I beg your pardon?" There was a slight but definite note of panic in the voice.

"I said, I think you should inform the police. I'm sure they'll be able to help you much better than I can." He paused. "If you really want to involve the law, that is."

Not a muscle of the man's face moved, but he was suddenly a different person. "What are you implying?" he asked calmly.

But Appy was not so easily tricked. "I'm implying nothing," he said. "Just making a sensible suggestion."

The man stood up and replaced his gloves. Then he said, almost sadly, "Think again, Mr Appleby. You may be making a big mistake."

Appy's hands tightened to fists inside his pockets. "I hope," he said, his voice steel-edged, "that you're not threatening me. Because if you are, someone will be contacting the police, even if you don't."

The stranger's hand was on the door handle. "I don't know what you mean," he said. He opened the door slightly. "But if I were you, I should be very careful."

He left as silently as he had come, and within seconds the fog had swallowed him. Appy was a stubborn man, but he was not stupid. He knew when to follow his instincts — and right now he was afraid.

The school secretary was busy: preparations for Christmas activities always began early. At the moment there were programmes for the annual carol concert to be typed and run off, and her fingers seemed never to leave the typewriter keys except during her lunch break.

As she was concentrating on a particularly bad example of the music teacher's handwriting, the phone rang. She let it. Jean, the other secretary, was down in the second office, sorting out dinner money, and her own hands were full. Whoever it was could phone back later, if it was that important.

The caller was persistent, but so was she. After another thirty seconds the ringing stopped.

It was lunchtime, but the bank of fog that smothered the plate glass of the dining room windows gave no indication of the hour. Since Simon had left the house at eight o'clock he had felt suspended in time, waiting for everything to move again. He was jarred out of his thoughts by a sudden sharp pain in his elbow. Matthew had just jabbed him with a fork.

"Wake up! You didn't hear a word I just said, did you?"

"Hm?"

"What are you going to do about the saxophone?"

Simon rubbed his wounded elbow. "Oh, nothing yet. Don't worry. It'll still be there for you to play at the weekend."

"Yes, but if it needs fixing . . . "

"Maybe it doesn't."

"But you know what that bloke said."

"Perhaps he's wrong. I bet you're more of an expert than him anyway." Flattery had always been one of Matthew's weak spots.

"You reckon?" Matthew adopted his expert-opinion face. "Well, I'll have more of an idea when I've seen it. Saturday morning be all right?"

"Fine."

Matthew returned, satisfied, to his lunch, leaving Simon alone to brood. He had tried not to think about the previous day's encounter but, without intending, he found himself increasingly wrapped in worry. On the surface he was his usual vague self, but inside there was a cold gnawing — a tension of the spirit that was barely concealed panic. He felt sure that he was teetering on the edge of something dangerous. And if he was on the edge, where did that leave Appy?

A buzzer sounded in the school office. The secretary lifted the internal phone and was greeted by the sound of the headmaster's harassed voice. "Mrs Jenkins, could I see you for a few minutes about the letter of invitation to the concert?"

"Certainly, Headmaster. I shan't be a moment."

She replaced the receiver and gazed in exasperation at Jean the second secretary. Carefully, she put down a half-eaten egg and cress sandwich next to her flask, licked her fingers, gathered up her notebook and pencil, and disappeared through an adjacent door into the headmaster's study. An illuminated panel immediately flashed the message 'Do not disturb' and Jean was left in charge.

Two minutes later the phone in the outer office rang. Keen to prove efficient, Jean answered immediately. "Roebuck School. Can I help you?"

"Good afternoon. Yes, I hope you can." It was a man's voice, polite but official. "I should like to contact one of your pupils, if possible. You see, I owe him something of a debt of gratitude. My little girl left home without her bus fare this morning. When she reached the bus stop she got into a bit of a panic, and if one of your lads hadn't given her the money she'd not have been able to get to school at all. My wife collected her for lunch, so we've only just discovered, and I thought I'd phone straight away to ask for his address."

Jean felt a little of the credit brush through her. The phone calls about pupils she had been unfortunate to answer tended to be much more irate: damage to garden fences, abuse and the occasional piece of shop-lifting. She was overdue for a compliment. "Well," she said reluctantly, "I'm not really supposed to give that sort of information."

"Oh, I do understand. It's just that my wife and I would greatly appreciate the chance to say thank you personally. My daughter said she thought his friends called him Bennett; er . . . Simon Bennett, I think."

She hesitated. Surely, under the circumstances there could be no harm. And think how pleased the Head would be to hear that one boy, at least, had done the school some credit. If she was in charge then she must show initiative.

"Hold on," she said. "I'll just see if I can find his record card."

*   *   *

As the afternoon progressed and the fog resolutely refused to lift, Simon's brooding turned to determination. Doing something, anything, would be preferable to feeling so useless. Fog or no fog, he must go back to Appy's. He had debated whether to tell Matthew but what could he say until he knew a few more facts himself?

When they met up in the cloakroom after the last lesson Matthew was in high spirits. He regaled Simon with the various jokes he had gathered during the day. So long as Simon reacted with a laugh or a groan in the appropriate place, Matthew was happy. In this fashion they plied their way through the murky air of the playground and out of the school gate, and it was not until they reached the main road that Simon found a chance to stem the flow of humour long enough to get a word in himself.

"Look," he said, stopping on the corner. "I don't think I'll catch the bus back with you today."

"Are my jokes that bad?" Matthew asked him.

"No — well, yes they are pretty bad."

"Thanks."

"But that's not the reason. I have to go into town."

Matthew looked properly aggrieved. "Fine," he said. "See if I care."

Simon could tell he was joking. He also knew that Matthew had probably guessed the truth but was too diplomatic to say. "Tell you what. I'll phone you later. OK?"

"With a proper explanation?"

"Yes." He didn't know yet whether he meant it, but it was the only thing he could say.

"See you then." Matthew turned on his heel and disappeared into the fog.

When Simon stepped off the bus in the city centre he began to wonder if it would be possible to find his way to the shop. All the landmarks he had previously used to guide himself there would be obscured. When he reached the small pond he stopped. Not only were his surroundings invisible, but no sounds penetrated to where he stood. He might be anywhere, or nowhere. Stifling this momentary sense of panic he pressed on in what he hoped was the right direction.

The lighted windows of the shop suddenly appeared, looking like beacons and taking him completely by surprise. He hurried across the street, remembering as he reached out for the door handle that he would have to use his weight. Nothing happened. He tried again and realised that this time the door was genuinely locked. He tapped the glass loudly then put his eye against it and peered through the condensation inside. A blurred figure appeared at the back of the shop but did not approach the door. It seemed pointless to knock again so Simon just waited. Eventually the blur grew larger and Appy's mittened hand wiped a circle on the glass, level with Simon's face. Their eyes met and it struck Simon that the old man's expression was a bizarre mixture of anxiety and relief.

The door swung open and Appy ushered him in. "Fancy seeing you," he said, and without waiting for Simon to reply led the way to the back of the shop. Outside the office he paused. "No. Upstairs, I think. It's more private."

A few days before, the idea of following this man anywhere would have seemed madness. Not any more. Simon trailed silently behind him up the wooden steps. Facing them at the top of the stairs was a door.

"In here," Appy said.

The room ran the full width of the building. It contained a large table, a settee and two armchairs but the first thing Simon noticed were the pictures. Every wall was covered with them: landscapes, portraits, still-lifes, sea pictures in oil and watercolour. He stared, open-mouthed.

"Take a look," Appy said. "Be my guest."

"I don't know where to start," Simon admitted.

Appy smiled. "That's a fair point. Well, if I go into a gallery what I always do is cast a quick look round, and if one of the pictures stands out I go and look at that one first. It's more interesting than ploughing your way dutifully round a wall." He stopped suddenly and laughed. Simon looked at him quizzically. "Sorry," he said. "Just remembering something that happened in a gallery in London."

"What was that?"

"American couple came in. I couldn't help hearing the conversation, they were talking so loud. Anyway, he insisted on buying the huge illustrated catalogue. 'We'd better have that,' he said. 'It'll have the pictures in.' I watched them. They walked right round the gallery and out again, and they didn't look at a single painting. She called out the numbers on the wall and he showed her the picture in the book. If I hadn't seen it with my own eyes I'd never have believed it."

If anyone other than Appy had told him, Simon wouldn't have believed it either. The old man indicated a place, far enough back from the wall, for him to stand. Simon positioned himself, closed his eyes, then opened them again. Immediately a small painting caught his attention, over in the far corner. He walked up to it. It was no brighter than any of the others and was dwarfed by the heavy gilt frames

94

around it, but it had stood out none the less. The subject was a sleeping child. Simon felt he was looking through a tiny window at the boy's head and the moonlight on the pillow.

"Ah," Appy said quietly, moving to join him. "I wondered if you'd choose that one."

"Why?" Simon asked him, surprised.

"You tell me first."

Simon considered. "It's got a sort of — atmosphere. Still and a bit mysterious. It reminds me of when I was little and I used to keep closing my eyes and opening them again because of the shadows in the room. I imagined all sorts of things hiding in the shadows. Scaring myself, I suppose."

Appy nodded. "That's very thoughtful," he said. "And honest."

"Why did *you* think I'd choose it?"

"Because it's the only one on that wall with a human figure in it. I thought you'd be more interested in a person than in trees or flowers."

"Yes," Simon said, and the look in his eyes changed. "There's something I want to ask you."

Appy gestured to the armchairs and they sat.

"Did you — have you told anyone else about the saxophone?" he asked. "Because yesterday a man, someone I'd never seen before, stopped me in the street. He said you wanted me to bring the saxophone back."

"Did he now? And what did he look like, this man?"

Simon told him and followed that with everything else he knew. Appy listened without interruption then said, "You're not the only one to be paid a visit. I've had two. Second one this morning. The first time he had another man with him."

"What do you think?" Simon asked him.

"I think you should get rid of that saxophone, and quickly."

"Take it to the police you mean?"

Appy shook his head. "I don't know."

"But — "

He held up his hand to keep Simon from continuing. "Right and wrong," he said. "That's what you're thinking isn't it? Right and wrong. I wish it was as simple as that, but sometimes doing what's right isn't the same thing as doing what's safe, because some people don't play by the rules. Do you get my meaning?"

Simon did. He thought of Mr Campbell beating boys in a little private room. That was nothing to what might happen in murky corners of the real world; and even Mr Campbell was not completely unscrupulous. "So what should we do?" he demanded.

Appy sighed. "Let me think about it," he said. "Maybe you're right about going to the police, after all. I don't know. Can you come back here tomorrow after school?"

Simon nodded.

"Good. And in the meantime, keep that saxophone safe. Got any friends you can really trust?"

"One."

"Perhaps you should tell him. Make sure you stick together when you're not at home."

"What about my parents?"

"You ought to tell them," Appy said. "But once you do that, it's out of your hands."

"I'll wait till tomorrow," Simon said. "Another day can't make much difference, can it?"

*   *   *

96

As evening fell, darkness soaked into the white air like filthy water into a bandage. It wrapped itself tight round the terraces near *Appleby's Antiques*, a tourniquet preventing movement. At ten everyone was indoors, waiting for clocks or televisions to tell them it was time to sleep.

Appy was upstairs, battling with income tax forms spread over the dining table. He had been putting off the dreary task for a week or more, but it would take his mind away from other things. He squinted. Deciphering lists of figures and small type through his old reading glasses was a feat that demanded all his concentration. It was no surprise, then, that the only movement for a mile around should have escaped his notice: the faint pad of two sets of footsteps on the pavement directly outside the shop. But the next sound flung him upright and out of his chair. The sound, or rather two in quick succession, was of the large windows to the front and side of the building shattering.

He had half expected something, but not this. Again he was a long way from the phone, but reaching it was a risk he would have to take. With luck, anyone throwing bricks would have run away, not followed them into the shop. He ran to the stairhead and peered down. The fumes and the noise told him: there would be no-one in the shop. It was worse than that. What had been hurled through the window was not bricks but petrol bombs.

By the time he reached the ground floor, furniture had already caught light. The whole shop, he realised with horror, was one huge tinder box: chairs, tables, books, horsehair sofas, all kindling for the spreading flames. The phone was no longer important. That could wait. First he must get out.

In his earlier anxiety he had not only double-locked the front door but wedged the largest of the heavy tables tight against it. As this was next to the front window it had caught the impact of the bomb, and was now ablaze. He had to get past the table if he was to escape. His only thought now was of getting out alive.

One end was still untouched by the flames. As he took hold of it he could feel the power of the heat on his face and forearms. He wrenched the clumsy piece of furniture round at an acute angle, but even as he did so the flames spurted suddenly up from around his feet, forcing him back into the shop.

He must think quickly. The windows were behind piles of furniture fast taking flame and he could not reach them without clambering over pieces already dangerously balanced. As he considered taking this risk at the side window a large oak sideboard, legs weakened by the fire, toppled forwards into a bookcase close by. Within minutes the whole of the ground floor would be burning. The air was suffocatingly close now, and the only clear retreat back up the stairs. Even the office, and its link with safety — the phone — was out of reach.

Shielding his eyes against the glare, Appy backed up the steps. He had no choice, but at least upstairs he could shut doors and delay the fire's progress until — hope and pray — people nearby had seen the inferno and sent for help. The only room with access from the street was his bedroom, so that was where he headed, coughing hard, his eyes stinging. Once inside he closed the door and leaned heavily against it.

Everything had happened so suddenly. Three minutes before, he had been in the room along the landing, bored and tired. Now he was fighting for his life. The problem was that everything depended on other people. Perched in this room, directly above the fire, he could do nothing to help himself. Or could he?

There was a sizeable ledge outside the window. If he was careful, he might be able to stand on it and pull himself on to the roof; the adjoining building should be safe from the blaze for a while yet.

He pushed up the sash window, to its highest point and eased himself into a straddling position half-in, half-out of the room. The fog, now tinged yellow from below, obscured the ground completely. He turned till he was facing back into the room and carefully hauled himself upright, keeping close against the solid comfort of the upper window. He did not want to lean into the invisible space behind any further than necessary.

His eyes were level with the eave of the roof and the struts supporting the guttering. Grasping hold of the metal trough he pulled slightly, testing it for strength. It seemed firm enough but what would happen when he subjected it to the full weight of his body? He stopped. Should he go back into the building and wait? As if in answer he heard a sudden roar and crackling, and the splintering of plaster, as part of the bedroom floor caved in where the heat below had grown too intense.

Summoning all his strength, he gripped tight with his fingers and levered himself upwards. If only his feet had something to reach for. The pressure was all on his arms and suddenly they felt pitifully old and weak. Perhaps if he broke the glass with his foot he could use the window frame for support. As he shifted his weight slightly to one side, his

fingers slipped on the crumbling inside edge of the gutter.
Before he had time even to scream, his hold was gone and
his body tumbled back into the night, twisting as it fell like a
diver, onto the hard surface of the concrete beneath.

Inside the building, ravaged and burning, his treasured
possessions began to curl and die.

Chapter Ten

In the middle of the night Simon woke, suppressing the scream that rose to his throat. He had fallen asleep with snatches of the taped music floating aimlessly through his head. It had not been an unpleasant feeling. As he slept, however, the music would not leave him but rose in intensity till it drowned all other sensations. He could smell hot, metallic air damp with breath, and suddenly the sound of the notes changed, turning into a harsh screech of human pain that ripped through his whole body.

Mercifully, it was at this point that he had woken, so abruptly that his heart jumped. For a while he lay, staring up at the ceiling, until his heart settled to its proper beat. There was an insistent stabbing in his brain that he had not felt since childhood. When he was four he had suffered from an ear infection which he had fought all one night, begging it to go away with tearless cries of frustration. Finally his father had come and, without a word, climbed into bed with him and stroked his head. In that reassuring presence he had felt the strength to cope. His father had stayed till morning and the pain had gone away.

The only remedy now was a dose of aspirin, and he made his way slowly and deliberately to the bathroom. The label on the bottle said one or two; he took two. Back on his bed he lay a long time with his eyes open. Gradually his eyelids relaxed.

When he woke next morning he felt strangely disconnected with the world. He knew he must have slept: his right arm was numb where he had been lying on it. But sleep had done nothing to refresh him. As soon as he appeared for breakfast his father commented on his appearance. "Good God," he said. "You look like you've had a night on the tiles."

"I should be so lucky." Simon managed a smile.

"Well," Mrs Bennett put in breezily. "If you're angling for a day off school I'm afraid you can't have it. I'm blitzing the house today."

"Bit early for a spring clean, isn't it?" her husband asked. "Or a bit late."

"It's never too late to try making this place more like home and less — " she looked pointedly at Simon " — like a sty."

"Are you all right?" asked Simon's father.

"Hm?" Simon looked up from the table. "Oh, I'm OK. But I wouldn't mind a lift to school if you're going that way."

Mrs Bennett grinned. "Nothing wrong with him," she said. "You fell straight into that."

Simon was glad she was making light of it. The unpleasant truth was that he had just remembered Appy's injunction to him not to go anywhere alone. He excused himself from the table and quickly gathered his school things together. Within five minutes they had left the house.

The ride to school was a silent one. Mr Bennett had never been one for enthusiastic chatter while he was driving, especially through early morning traffic. Simon watched the scenery slide past. Out there, he thought; somewhere out there — but he tried to concentrate on other, ordinary things. Lesson two there would be a Maths test, and he had done no revision. But however hard he tried, he could not make that fact seem important.

His father dropped him near the school gates. "Take care," he said as Simon was closing the car door. "You still look a bit wobbly."

"Thanks, Dad. I will."

The car pulled away and disappeared round the corner.

Matthew was rather less concerned about Simon's appearance: he had other things on his mind. "Thank you very much," he said testily as Simon sat next to him in registration.

"What?"

"I really enjoyed the long, informative phone call last night. It made my evening." Simon continued to look puzzled. "You said you'd phone me," Matthew said in a tone of weary patience like a teacher talking to a particularly slow child.

"Oh, I'm sorry. I forgot."

"Bloody hell. Can't you come up with something a bit more inspiring than that? 'I forgot'!"

"Well I did. What else am I supposed to say?"

"I don't know. How about 'My great Aunt Nelly suddenly popped off and we had to fly to Australia to pick up the body'?"

"What's got into you this morning?" Simon asked him.

"Oh, nothing. I just thought you might have been doing something important enough to forget your best friend, that's all."

"Maybe I was."

"Fine. I hope you enjoyed it." He lapsed into moody silence and Simon did not have the energy to pull him out of it. As it happened, Matthew's huffiness concealed a genuine worry, but he did not know how to put it into words.

It was a silly argument, but it served to separate them. They stayed like that for the rest of the day and anything they wished to say remained unspoken. So it was that, despite his own misgivings, Simon left after school with a crowd of other boys heading for the city centre. He managed to convince himself that at least while he was with them he could come to no harm. Once he left the bus station and set off for *Appleby's Antiques*, he would just have to trust to luck.

Simon's stop was nearly a quarter of a mile from his house and, as he climbed down from the bus, he was by no means certain of making it. His leg muscles seemed to act independently of his brain, giving him the uneven gait of a drunken man. His breathing was shallow. Closing his eyes he could believe he was a climber at altitude, rather than walking the same route he had taken for the past three years.

For the last half hour it had rained solidly. Now it stopped abruptly. Dusk distorted the surroundings: the sky, which had a short while ago been grey, was now the deep, glowing blue of ink in a glass bottle; cars cast black reflections on the wet road; the silhouette fingers of trees were darker than the sky they leaned on; and in the middle distance streetlights shimmered and sparkled, oscillating in the damp air.

Simon rubbed his eyes, trying to focus his concentration. If anything, that made matters worse. Pictures of the shop he had just left snapped up in front of him — charred walls, smashed and boarded-up windows, and the collapsed and caved-in roof. How could something so solid, so permanent, be destroyed so quickly?

The evening before he had been there: walked through the shop, crowded with furniture the same way it had been for years. He had stood in the private room upstairs, surrounded by rows of paintings and talking with Appy. Appy. He had tried to keep thoughts of him completely out of his mind. He refused even to imagine what might have happened, or where Appy might be at that moment.

By now he was at the end of his own road. He could not remember walking there; it had just happened. He turned the corner, unaware of the footsteps behind him.

"Excuse me."

He stopped. What did they want? Maybe he'd dropped something from his bag while walking in that daze. He turned round. A man in a camel-hair coat, hands in pockets, was strolling towards him.

Simon took one look and ran. The man made no move to follow.

Halfway down the road another figure stepped out from the end of a drive. Simon gave up. He nearly sat down on the pavement: he was physically and mentally exhausted. Instead, he put his bag down and leaned back into the hedge of the nearest garden.

The men were in no hurry. They sauntered up and stood just in front of him, one each side. Simon looked from one to the other. It was the elder who spoke.

"Hello, young man. I don't think you stuck to your promise, did you?"

"What do you mean?" There was probably no point in

playing for time; they'd stand there as long as they liked. But it seemed the easiest form of resistance.

"You know what I'm talking about." The voice was exaggeratedly patient. "The saxophone — remember?"

"What about it? It doesn't need repairing, if that's what you mean."

"Oh dear." He turned imploringly to the younger man, like an exasperated parent, then took one short step towards Simon and thrust an open hand over his face, pushing him back into the hedge. He held him there for several seconds while Simon struggled, then grabbed him by his coat and thrust him at the other man. Simon felt two steel claws grasp the top of his arms, pinning them to his body. Camel-hair leaned close to him.

"I really did think you were a bright lad," he said. "Not a little idiot who wants to play silly and dangerous games."

Simon tried to twist away but the claws tightened.

"But of course, you are, aren't you — a bright lad? That's why I'm not wasting any more time making up stories to tell you. I'm sure facts impress you much more. So when you get home take a look at your evening paper. You'll find an article about a fire in a certain shop we both know."

"You . . . ?" Simon had no need to finish the sentence.

"Oh, so you know about that already. Well, I'm sure I need say no more. That's a nice house you live in — you and your parents — and we all want it to stay that way. So it will, if you do the right thing. I want the saxophone, in its case, out here within the next fifteen minutes. Do I make myself clear?"

There were many things Simon wanted to say, but he would have choked on all of them.

Cold eyes stared unblinkingly at him. "I said, *Is* that clear?"

Simon nodded slowly.

"Good. And to make it all square we'll settle up with you quite generously." He tapped the breast pocket containing his wallet, then nodded to the other man. Simon found himself roughly released. He massaged his shoulders to get some feeling back into them. Without a word he picked up his bag and moved off.

His mother was on the phone when he opened the front door. "Hang on," she said into the receiver. "It's Simon." She cupped her hand over the mouthpiece. "Tea's in the kitchen. Stick the kettle on; I shan't be a minute." Then she resumed her conversation.

Once in the kitchen, Simon put his bag down and reached for the kettle. This was crazy. What was he doing? Appy's shop had been set on fire, the men responsible were outside waiting for him and here he was making a pot of tea. Was it possible for comfortable routine and horror to live side by side? He remembered a television programme he'd seen, about the lives of ordinary German civilians during the Second World War. Parish meetings had been held in the village hall to discuss defective street lighting, while half a mile away on the railway lines trucks crammed with other human beings were rumbling towards the concentration camps. But you always thought it happened somewhere else or in another time, not on your own doorstep.

The evening paper was on the table. He didn't have to search far: it was the main item of news. FIRE DEMOLISHES CITY SHOP. He skimmed hurriedly through for news of Appy. ' . . . *taken to County Hospital* . . . *critical condi-*

tion.' So he hadn't been killed. That was the great fear Simon had tried so hard to suppress. Despite what was happening around him he felt a surge of relief.

His mother came into the kitchen. "That was your dad. Two months I've been trying to persuade him to take me out for a meal and at long last he's done something about it. I think he must have run out of jobs to do."

"When are you going?"

"About half-past seven. He's got a table booked for eight-fifteen."

Simon looked surprised. "What? Tonight?"

"No, dear. Next week. We're going to camp out on the pavement to make sure of getting a table. It's a busy place."

Normally Simon would have groaned loudly, but tonight he said nothing. His mother was quick to notice.

"What's up with you?"

Here was his opportunity to tell her, but his brain was still numb and he just shook his head. "Nothing — chlorine in my eyes." The explanation seemed to satisfy her and she began bustling round as a preliminary to getting changed for her evening out.

Simon wandered upstairs and pulled aside the curtains in the front bedroom. Beyond the shadows cast by walls and hedges he could see two more, quite distinctly. How much longer had he got? He'd not been keeping track of the time. Common sense told him he must give the two men what they wanted. Then, with the immediate danger past, he would tell his parents, and together they'd inform the police.

He went back to his own room and took the heavy black case from its hiding place in the wardrobe.

Then he remembered the tape. Did they know about that? Was that maybe what they were really after? He could not conceive how the saxophone was so important to them. A tape — that made more sense. If so, maybe he could play for time after all; pretend he knew nothing about it and just hand over the saxophone. He thought of that oily voice and its warning. It wasn't worth the risk.

Reluctantly he picked up the box with the tape in and was about to put it back into the case. The cassette was as he had left it, at the end of the first side. Of course. He'd only listened to one side, assuming the silence at the end to mean there was nothing more on it. But there could be anything at all on the other side. He wanted to listen; to find out. But there was thirty minutes' playing time and, at most, he had five minutes to return to the waiting figures.

He moved to the front room again. A quick look told him they were still there. Would they really go if he was late? Surely they'd wait until he came. It was too important for them not to. That meant he could keep them waiting out in the cold for a while yet. He had what they wanted; that gave him a certain power. They were just trying to panic him into not realising his advantage.

It had been a difficult decision to make but he felt grimly determined. Returning to his room he placed the tape carefully in the cassette player and sat down on the edge of the bed. For a long time there was nothing; he was tempted to jump ahead but forced himself to be patient. He'd heard the other side right through. He must do the same with this one.

After ten minutes his mother called him downstairs, insisting she'd throw his tea away if he didn't come down and have it there and then. This was no time for a row. He clicked the tape to a stop and went back to the front window.

Outside, the road was full of shadows, but two were missing. He could not believe it. How could he have been so mistaken? Maybe they'd just returned to the car, out of the cold for a while. He hurried downstairs and hastily downed a cup of tea and a couple of sandwiches. His mother was in the living room saving her appetite for later.

When he looked out again there was still no trace of the men. Whatever happened now he had plenty of time to hear the rest of the tape.

For the next twenty minutes Simon listened with increasing despair. When he removed the cassette his hands were shaking. There had been nothing, no recognisable sound at all except the constant hissing of blank tape. The risk he had taken had been totally pointless — 'a silly and dangerous game'. Those twenty minutes had given him more than enough time to catalogue the very real dangers involved.

His father would be home in a while, and in two hours his parents would leave the house. He must tell them as soon as possible. But there was so much to say. Where should he begin? He had never been very good at sharing feelings or personal problems with them. And, anyway, if he was turning to them for comfort and reassurance, like a small child with a grazed knee, they would be powerless to provide it. Against such men they could do no more than he. It would be simpler and more straightforward to go to the police alone after his parents had left. The saxophone — and the tape, for what that was worth — could stay at home; he already had a safe place of concealment worked out for them.

But most important of all, before he went anywhere else, he must find out about Appy. He felt sure there was no chance he'd be told anything over the phone so he'd have to go in person. By the time his parents returned home he would have been both to the hospital and to the police. Then he, and his parents, would sleep more easily.

He unclasped the black case, placed the cassette on the dark velvet, and lifted out the precious instrument. His fingers traced the maze of lines on its smooth surface. At the centre they found the tiny initials. If anyone could explain why all this had to happen, it was Calvin Stephens.

And he was two years silent.

Chapter Eleven

The hospital was a large, imposing monument of Victorian red brick approached by a semi-circular drive. At the front, alongside the pavement, ran a tall laurel hedge, broken where the drive began and ended by two wrought iron gateways. The gates themselves had long since disappeared: visiting relatives may well have admired them when the hospital was built, but negotiating them in a car caused too many problems. By now a one-way system had also been introduced, so that the gate under which Simon now stood not only carried a weathered shield, embossed with the arms of the county, but a large blue and white notice saying EXIT ONLY. An arrow pointed along the hedge, some thirty yards, to the second gate. As a pedestrian he could have used either, but he followed the arrow anyway.

The firm resolve which had led him there was slipping. He was already soaked through and though it had now stopped raining, he hardly noticed. The hedge cascaded water onto his shoulder as he brushed against it. Damn! Standing there shivering wasn't helping anyone. He reached the second gate and strode as briskly as he could towards the entrance.

Once under the porch he shook the worst of the water from his hair before climbing the steps to the large swing doors into reception. The porter at the desk looked up. Simon blinked away a drop of water that had trickled from his forehead and cleared his throat.

"Could you tell me what ward Mr Appleby's in? He was admitted last night, I think."

The porter frowned. "Bit late for visiting aren't you?"

"I only found out an hour ago and I came over straight away." Hoping he could sound convincing, he launched into his prepared speech. "I was told he was in intensive care. Doesn't that mean you can visit at any time?"

"That depends." The porter leaned his elbow on the desk. "If he's not well enough for visitors then *no-one's* allowed to see him. And, anyhow, people don't normally just turn up out of the night. We know when they're coming. Did you phone the hospital first?"

Simon was non-plussed by this piece of cold logic. "Well . . . no. I thought, as it was serious, I ought to get here as quick as I could."

"You a relative of this Mr . . . "

"Appleby. No, but it's very important. I must see him."

All pretence had gone from Simon now. It seemed impossible to bluff his way any further. "He'll want to see me — I know he will. Please!"

The face on the other side of the counter softened a little. "All right, don't get so worked up. I'll see what I can find out." He headed towards the phone then turned back to Simon. "Was he the one badly hurt in that fire?"

"Yes," Simon said quietly.

"Ah." The porter looked down at the floor. "Look, you just sit over there and I'll get someone to come and see you. All right?" He pointed to a row of metal and canvas chairs in the entrance hall. Simon nodded.

The chairs were next to the main staircase and when he sat down his back was to the reception desk. He examined his surroundings. The main feature of the hallway was the huge stone staircase that began next to him and wound its way round three walls, up to the first floor landing. Its heavy iron banister was a scaled-down version of the missing entrance gates, stretched out like a concertina. As he craned his neck backwards, Simon could see a small, round skylight some four storeys up. Faintly, rain began to spatter against the glass. He was going to get soaked again.

He lowered his head and gazed around the hallway. Opposite was a kiosk with gifts and sweets, closed now; to his left, a public phone, and over on the other side a lift. It appeared very small, hardly adequate to transport visitors, staff, trolleys and stretchers. Where was the lift at the moment? He glanced at the numbers above the door. First floor. Over his shoulder he could see the porter engaged in earnest conversation.

Without being quite sure of what he was doing, Simon stood quietly up and moved stealthily across the marble tiles to the lift. He pressed the button. The porter looked up suddenly, spoke a few quick words into the phone and hurriedly left the desk.

"Hang on a minute," he was saying as he advanced, and then the lift door opened and Simon stepped in. He found the button marked 'third floor' and thumped it hard. Nothing happened, and now the porter was running. Simon hit the button again and slowly the door began to close, blocking the porter from view. There was a shout, then a loud click from outside, but the lift was on the move.

What would the porter do? Sprint up the stairs? Phone someone to intercept him? Simon had no idea where he was going. He hadn't even seen a sign to indicate the wards. It eemed a lifetime before the lift finally jolted to a stop on the third floor.

When he emerged he found himself facing a broad balcony that ran right round the stairwell. Leaning over the railings, he could just make out the row of seats where he had been waiting. Mercifully, there was no sound of rushing feet on the stairs, but he felt exposed where he was and looked around for an alternative route.

Next to the lift was a small swing door and, behind that, a narrow flight of stairs to the one remaining floor of the building. It turned a corner round the back of the lift shaft and there Simon took off his anorak and sat down on the steps to think. Finally, discomfort, more than any clear plan, drove him to find somewhere to dry himself.

The top floor was cramped, with narrow corridors and the climate of a hothouse. He turned right, past a large plate of reinforced glass which looked out over the hospital roof. Beyond, he saw the lights of the city centre and the high-rise blocks with their ribbons of windows, some bright, others in darkness. At the end of the corridor he found what he was searching for: a door marked 'Toilet — Staff Only'. No-one had emerged from the small wards abutting the corridor to challenge him, so he sidled in and locked the door. He used half the automatic hand towel before he felt vaguely dry again, but his trousers still stuck unpleasantly to his legs.

His original impulse had been to search until he found Appy, but it now dawned on him how futile such a search would be. There were so many wards that he could never hope to find the right one by himself. He'd been an idiot to run away in the first place. The most sensible thing to do was go back to reception and ask again. That way he'd at

least find out what state Appy was in. Retracing his steps t
the top of the main staircase, he clattered down, anora
over his shoulder.

It was only as he turned the last curve in the staircase tha
he spotted the two men talking to the porter, and thoug
they had their backs to him there was no mistaking thei
identity. The overhead light picked out a head of smooth
greying hair, turning it momentarily silver.

Instantly Simon froze and pressed his back to the wall
Had they come for him or to complete their unfinishec
business with Appy? He couldn't hear what they wer
saying, but he could guess. Still against the wall anc
watching for any sign of movement from the men, he easec
his way back up the stairs. He had gone six steps before hi
heel caught the next tread and he stumbled noisily.

The younger man turned towards the stairs. Immediately
he grabbed the other's shoulder and pointed. Simon was a
prisoner caught on the wrong side of the wire, in the ful
glare of the searchlights. He turned, and scrambled up the
steps to the next floor. Glancing back he saw the first man
reach the bottom of the stairs. The other had moved to the
lift door and was watching him dispassionately.

Simon nearly tripped again as he reached the landing. His
nerves were screaming. Where could he run to? Every door
had a stranger behind it; every corridor was a threat. If he
just spiralled upwards he would run out of space.

Then, out of nowhere, one clear thought arrived. If all the
floors were built on the same plan . . . He hurled himself
bodily down the passage to his left. Yes! There was the
door: 'Staff Only'. He was inside so fast he nearly cannoned
into the washbasin. Bolting the door, he waited as silently as

e could. His whole body seemed to be full of noises: heart pounding, blood thudding in his ears, his breathing dislocated.

It all depended on timing. Had he managed to disappear from view before his pursuer rounded the bend in the stairs? If so, he might yet be safe. Or had he been seen heading down the corridor? If that had happened . . . He imagined a figure, two figures, outside propped patiently against the wall, waiting.

He listened, concentrating every ounce of his hearing into the corridor. Nothing could be heard: not even the faint scuffle of a shoe or a tell-tale whisper of clothing.

He stayed frozen for two minutes. All he needed was a bit of luck. It took him half a minute more to ease the door gently open, far enough to look back along the corridor. From the darkness of the toilet, it seemed far brighter than when he had left it. The dull enamelled walls had acquired a luminous sheen.

No-one was there. He put on his anorak and stepped out.

Though he tried to move quietly, by the time he reached the staircase a desire to run had overwhelmed him. Clutching the banister, he propelled himself, half running, half jumping down the stairs. He jarred his knee as he hit the bottom, but there was no time to find out if it hurt. The lift was descending, the door opening.

As Simon pelted past the alarmed porter he could hear two pairs of feet in the marble hallway. Arms in front of him he crashed through the swing doors. They drummed back and forth behind him, drowning the porter's shouts. He cleared the steps and was across the lawn to the end of the drive in seconds, skidding into the rain-swept street.

From outside the hospital entrance Simon could already hear the loud revving of a car's engine.

Chapter Twelve

For one moment he nearly seized up with panic. He was already gasping for breath, and his left knee seemed quite badly twisted. Only in his worst dreams had he ever felt like this before: trapped in slow-motion flight and too afraid to look back. But in a dream, when he felt something brush the back of his heels, the hot breath on his neck, he knew he would soon wake up. It would all be over. Not this time; not when he was already awake.

He dared a look behind and saw the beam of the headlights dip as they neared the gate. Gathering his breath, he plunged towards the city centre. How long could he keep this up? He had no idea, but unless he tried he was a sitting target.

There was a screech of brakes. Simon punched his feet on the pavement, nearly toppling forwards in his determination to keep moving. Adjusting his balance, he was aware of the car accelerating into the road. It would take them seconds to pull level with him; no more.

Twenty metres ahead was a sturdy metal railing, designed to prevent people taking a short cut across four lanes of speeding traffic on the ring road. Simon concentrated on the top bar of the railing, calculating how best to clear it. Out of the corner of his eye he caught the flickering image of the approaching car.

He almost changed his mind. To his right was a flight of

steps leading down to the underpass. He hovered next to them for a split second. No. That's where they'd expect him to go. On the ring road he had at least half a chance. He grabbed the metal bar and hoisted himself up far enough to put one foot on the top. Then he swung over and dropped to the other side.

Traffic shot past him. If he could just get across and along the opposite side there was no way they'd reach him in the car. They'd be forced to abandon it and follow on foot. He'd not heard the car doors open yet; they must be waiting to see what he'd do. He found himself clinging to the railings in the same way he used to hug the rail in the swimming baths when he first learnt to swim. Frantically he searched for a gap in the traffic flow, then could wait no longer and flung himself desperately out into the road.

An oncoming van sounded its horn but stayed on course. Had it swerved, he would have been under it, for by now he was in the outside lane. Once on the central reservation he checked quickly left then ran fast to the far railings and swarmed over them. His knee clipped the top bar and this time he felt a definite, sharp pain that made him gasp aloud.

Only when he was on the pavement did he look back again. There was the car parked at the junction, avoiding the turn which would take it in the wrong direction — away from the fleeing figure. But there was only one person in it.

Simon scanned the far side of the road for the second man, expecting to see him by the railings, or even over them by now. But there was no sign of him. He couldn't just have vanished. Where . . . ? Then Simon remembered: down and through the underpass, the route he nearly took himself, aiming to cut him off as he headed down the pavement.

That's what *they* thought! At the moment *he* had the upper hand and he intended to keep it that way.

He climbed carefully back over the railings, lifting the damaged knee well above the top bar. Then he started to run in the same direction as the passing traffic. Fifty metres further on there was another intersection, this time bigger and busier. He would have to decide in advance what to do when he reached it; if only he knew where the man tracking him had gone.

As if in answer he heard a yell somewhere behind him. The driver must be pointing him out to the other man. Perhaps he should cut back over the road, but that still made it just a matter of time before he tired and slowed to a standstill.

Cars began to slow as they neared the intersection. Simon felt the air of their slipstream; a door handle nearly brushed his arm. Of course! It was worth a try. Casting a quick glance over his shoulder he put out his hand, thumb raised and began hitching for a lift as he ran.

Three cars passed him as if he wasn't there. The driver of the fourth, an old and battered sports car, turned to look at him but seemed about to ignore him as well. Simon had no intention of letting him. He waved his arms furiously as the driver looked in his mirror. Immediately, the left-hand indicator flashed and the car pulled to a halt a short way ahead. Simon prayed it wouldn't take too long to persuade him but the man swung the door open straight away. He was inside and the car moving away before either he or the driver spoke.

"That lunatic anything to do with you?" The driver gestured towards the back windscreen. Framed in the glass was the top half of a man who now lunged at the aerial on the wing of the car. Simon felt he could have reached out and touched him. There was a metallic thud and Simon held his breath.

"Bloody idiot," grunted the driver. He put his foot hard on the accelerator, checked the mirror and stuck two fingers up triumphantly. The flailing figure outside receded from view as they entered the roundabout.

"Right, squire. Where are you headed for?"

Simon suddenly realised he had no idea of their direction. He told the driver his address. "If that's not too far out of your way," he added.

"Sure, that's fine." The driver reached in his pocket for a cigarette and waved the packet in Simon's direction. "Smoke?"

He almost said yes. After all, weren't they supposed to calm your nerves? But he was breathless enough already. He indicated no, half closed his eyes and watched the streetlights sweep past, each one putting more distance between him and the men in the grey car.

It took them less than a minute to break in. A brief phone call had convinced them: there might be a light on downstairs but no-one was at home. After a cursory check downstairs they sought out Simon's room. Expert eyes and fingers pried into corners, beneath the bed, and then turned to the wardrobe.

The sliding door creaked stiffly on its runners; hands closed round coats, trousers, cardboard boxes crammed with odds and ends. Unsuccessful, they moved to the cupboard above. There was no saxophone case.

An exasperated voice cracked the silence. "Well, where now? We going to search the whole bloody house?"

"No." Mr Schaeffer sat down on the bed. He took off his coat, brushed off droplets of water, and folded it neatly. He placed it on the covers beside him. "We're going to wait."

Even though it must have taken him a good mile and a half off his route, the driver dropped Simon right at the end of his road. "Don't worry about it," he said. "Life's too short to worry." It was not a comment likely to boost Simon's confidence and he hurried between the separate pools of streetlight, keen to get back into the house and close the door.

In the hallway he stopped by the phone. The sooner he called the police the better, then they could come and collect the saxophone and he would tell them everything: talk and talk until his throat dried up; make amends for keeping silent too long. But first he needed to get something warm inside him. He had begun to shiver.

He plugged in the kettle then went through to the living room and switched on the television. That way he would feel less alone in the house. When he returned to the kitchen he found himself shivering again. It felt even colder there than it had in the other room. He looked round and his eye caught a small piece of glass on the draining board. It was unlike either of his parents to break something and not to clear up the pieces. He picked it up. The temperature was coldest where he stood. The bottom of the curtain moved. He pulled it back and wind gusted through a gaping hole in the glass. The cold slid down his spine.

And suddenly he found himself listening. The television.

Where was the sound of the television? Maybe . . . there must be a break in the programme. Any moment now the adverts would start. By now he was holding his breath. Nothing. He began to turn around.

"Hello, Simon."

The voice came from just outside the door to the hallway.

Simon made a noise in his throat, then aloud, as the first figure appeared. "Have you finished playing now?" the man said. "Are you going to be sensible? Because I'm getting very tired — and angry."

Mr Schaeffer pulled a kitchen chair from beneath the table and sat, facing Simon. He formed his words slowly and deliberately. "For the last time, where is it?"

The other man was in the doorway now.

Simon had no resistance left. He would have told them anything, everything, but fear made him mute. He simply could not speak.

Mr Schaeffer stood up. Without warning his clenched fist slammed against Simon's head, spinning him sideways. He fell against the sink. Before he reached the floor powerful hands pulled him back up and something like a hammer landed in his stomach. His breathing stopped. He wanted to be sick. He collapsed to the floor, kneeling, his head against the cold tiles, hands clutching his stomach. Again he was hauled upwards, like a drowning man surfacing for the last time.

"I've had enough of you," a muffled voice was saying somewhere close to his ear. "And I don't care if you can't speak to me: I wouldn't believe a word you said anyway. You're a lying little bastard and you're going to suffer for it, but first — " His voice acquired a playful tone. "You are going to take us and show us where you put the big black case."

Had he not been held up, Simon would have been unable to walk at all. He moved unsteadily to the back door. It was unlocked for him. Then he led them through the yard towards the passage that ran down the side of the house. At the corner he was stopped.

"A word to the wise, Simon. If you're thinking of getting back out the front where people can see you, forget it. I'll personally smash your head against the wall before you're halfway through the gate. Understand?"

Simon wanted to lie down and go to sleep. He nodded vaguely.

"Fine. Now move."

The passage was dark. There was a light on the wall further up but the switch was in the house and he had forgotten to press it. He stumbled, losing his footing on the wet paving stones. Straight away he was forced upright. The journey seemed to take minutes, but finally he stopped near the gate. They were standing by the dustbin.

"Very smart, Simon. Now open it."

He did so.

"Take out the case."

He bent over and tried to lift it but blood rushed to his head and he sat down in a heap by the dustbin.

It was left to the younger man to collect it. Simon could hear him flip the catch. He turned his head; saw him kneeling down; the dull glint of gold as the case was opened. He was aware of the legs and feet of the man in front of him, and of one foot lifting slowly, moving backwards frame by frame, a film slowed to its lowest crawling speed. And then noises: feet running, a loud voice . . .

With a snap the film broke and Simon was back in the dark.

Chapter Thirteen

The darkness stayed. Simon floated in it, all sensations dead. He couldn't even dream. Time itself had stopped.

A voice.

"Simon. Simon, can you hear me?"

He could not — or he did not want to.

The darkness continued.

Which part of his brain came back to life first, he could not afterwards have said. Did everything perhaps return at once? For suddenly he could see a cream ceiling and hear the sound of people moving somewhere below him.

As he turned his head on the pillow a wardrobe door came in to focus. Part of him said: "I'm waking up in my bedroom but I don't remember going to sleep."

He thought about this carefully, closed his eyes again and tried to remember. Random pieces of information registered, then vanished.

His head hurt.

He fell asleep.

When he awoke for the second time he realised it was light outside; too light for early morning. He'd better get up.

He dropped his legs over the side of the bed and stood.

Funny. His body felt unusual, as if it didn't belong to him. Light-headed, he put his hand on the bed to steady himself. Abruptly he sat down, his foot thumping hard against the radiator by the bed.

"Simon?" The voice came from downstairs.

"Yes." His own voice sounded too loud; he hadn't meant to shout.

He could hear footsteps on the stairs — hurrying. The door opened and his mother stood there. Why was she looking so worried?

"Simon, are you all right?"

He smiled queasily. "Mm . . . I think so."

Next moment his mother was sitting beside him and he was surprised to find himself being hugged. Just as suddenly she let go, as if he were some delicate object she was afraid to damage. Then Simon noticed her eyes. Was she starting to cry?

"Mum, what's up?"

"You don't remember?"

He looked blank. "Remember what?"

His mother took a deep breath. "Right," she said. "Tell me your name."

"Huh."

"Never mind why. Just tell me: what's your full name?"

He shrugged. "Simon Bennett."

"What about your middle name?"

He pulled a face. "George. Simon George Bennett." He'd been given his grandfather's name and it had always embarrassed him.

"What date's your birthday?"

"August the tenth. What are you doing this for?"

"One more, Simon. What did you get for your birthday? What did your dad and I buy for you?"

He smiled. "A pair of headphones so you wouldn't be disturbed when I wanted to play my music too loud."

She smiled too, then hugged him again. "Go on. Back into bed for now."

Simon was beginning to get cross. "Why? You haven't told me what's going on. Why are you playing this game?"

"It's not a game, love. Do you remember anything about the night before last?"

He thought, and she could tell by the puzzled expression on his face what the answer was.

"No, I thought not. Don't worry: that's no bad thing."

She helped him back under the covers and tucked them in, then sat on the edge of the bed. "The night before last, a doctor asked you the same questions at the hospital. You couldn't answer any of them, not even your name, so they kept you in overnight for observation. Now your memory's come back you've lost the time from before. The doctor told us that's what should happen. Thank goodness it has."

"But why was I in hospital?"

Gently his mother reached up and touched the side of his head. For the first time since waking he realised there was something there. He felt for it gingerly. It was a bandage and around it he could feel that some of his hair had been cut away. He opened his mouth to speak.

"Stitches," his mother said. "Five of them." She put her finger to her lips. "Now, no more questions. Just you rest."

She left the room and closed the door quietly. Soon Simon was aware of her voice downstairs. It drifted over him in a soft wave. Why hadn't he asked what time it was?

As he fell back to sleep he heard the phone start to ring.

*   *   *

"Mum?"

In half a minute she was there.

"What's the time?"

"Half-past twelve. Midday," she added. "How would you like some breakfast?"

Normally his mother was irritated if he wasn't down for breakfast by eight o'clock, even at weekends, but he wasn't going to argue. He was very hungry.

"Yes please. Oh, and what day is it? Is it Saturday?"

"Spot on, Brains. I can see you're well on the way to recovery. By the way, when you've had your breakfast do you fancy seeing a visitor?"

"Visitor?"

"Young man by the name of Matthew. He's waiting at home like a cat on hot bricks next to the phone. Anyone would think you were pregnant!"

Simon laughed, then stopped as it boomed around the inside of his head. He winced.

"That'll hurt for a while yet, but at least you're back in the land of the living. Shall I tell him he can come round then?"

Simon ventured a cautious smile. "I thought it was me that had just come round."

His mother groaned. "You're back to normal," she said and set off to prepare a large, healthy breakfast.

Considering the person on the landing had pounded up the stairs like a hippopotamus in a hurry, the tiny tap on the bedroom door was comical.

Simon smiled. "Come in."

Matthew peered nervously round the edge of the door. "How are you feeling?" he whispered.

Simon was by now propped up with a pillow behind him. "You don't need to overdo it," he said. "I'm not about to kick the bucket."

Matthew relaxed. "Good, because the other night . . . " He looked guiltily over his shoulder towards the door. "Oh. I mean . . . I promised your mum not to upset you or anything." His concern for the invalid in the bed was fighting a losing battle with his natural eagerness to talk.

Simon decided to help out. "I don't think you can really do much harm by talking to me."

It was the cue Matthew had been waiting for. He came round to the side of the bed and sat on the window-sill. "Thursday night," he said. "I kept trying to phone you but there was no answer, and I knew there was something wrong, what with you being all buried in yourself. I sort of wanted to apologise too, about us falling out at school, and, of course, I was hoping to see the saxophone . . . "

Something clicked in Simon's mind. He was no longer certain he wanted to listen, but Matthew was ploughing on regardless. " . . . and then I saw the evening paper, and there it was on the front page. Appleby. And I remembered that was the name the bloke outside the school said to you."

Simon remembered now. For a while he was completely unaware of Matthew's voice as he grappled with what was happening inside his head. His brain was bombarded by a series of images, each one more unpleasant than the last, and it was all he could do to stop himself from shouting aloud. When he re-emerged Matthew was saying " . . . so in the end I persuaded Dad to come round here and wait for you to come back. Only you already were."

He shook his head philosophically. "It was lucky we came when we did, in time to stop you getting your head kicked in even worse."

Simon grimaced. "You're nothing if not graphic," he said.

"Sorry." Matthew looked genuinely shamefaced. "Do you want me to finish?"

"You may as well," Simon reassured him. "After all, you're only telling the truth."

"All right, but the thing is: they got away — whoever it was who was attacking you. As soon as Dad sprinted up the drive shouting, they ran. Dad nearly caught one of them. He'd got the saxophone case, Dad said, and it slowed him down. Actually, I reckon it's a good thing he didn't get hold of him. He'd probably have come off worse. He didn't even see their faces. Who was it? Was it the bloke we saw outside school?"

Simon was not listening. His mind had returned to the single most important memory that had surfaced. He ignored Matthew's question in an attempt to phrase one of his own.

"Do you know what's happened — How's Mr Appleby?"

There was a sound of footsteps on the stairs, heralding the end of the visit. Matthew stared hard out of the window.

Mrs Bennett came in. She looked at the two boys. "What? Finished talking already? That's not like you, Matthew."

Matthew tried to smile but succeeded only in looking even more uncomfortable.

"Mum?"

She turned to Simon.

"What's happened to Mr Appleby? Do you know?"

Mrs Bennett understood. She glanced sympathetically towards Matthew. It wasn't fair that he should have to answer. She sat on the bed and took Simon's hand.

"I'm sorry, love," she said softly. "We found out at the hospital. Somebody said you'd been looking for him."

Simon turned his head away but that did not stop his mother speaking the words, nor himself hearing them.

"He died yesterday morning."

Music filled Mr Schaeffer's living room: the music of a saxophone. After a while Mr Schaeffer left the comfort of his armchair by the fire to remove the tape from the cassette deck. Jarrod looked up at him in surprise. "That's it?" he said. "This tape's what it was all about?"

"Don't you like the music?"

"Not much."

Mr Schaeffer smiled expansively as he sat down again. "You are a philistine," he said.

Jarrod grew visibly more agitated. "Don't tell me we went through all this just to listen to music."

"Not just anybody's music." The voice had an air of mockery. "We have the pleasure of listening to a young man named Calvin Stephens."

Jarrod scowled.

"Let me put it this way," Mr Schaeffer said. "There is something else on the tape but not in the way you would expect." He juggled the cassette reflectively in his hand. "Perhaps you were hoping to hear some sort of incriminating conversation. If so, I'm sorry to disappoint you. Here, catch!"

He threw the tape to the other man who, reacting quickly, caught it in his large fingers. He peered closely at the outer casing, turning it this way and that, but his look of puzzlement remained.

"None the wiser? Throw it back then."

Mr Schaeffer snapped it back into its plastic box and his smile broadened. "Now we've both handled it. The only difference is, that in your case this was the first time."

Gradual understanding dawned on Jarrod's face. "You mean — ?"

"Exactly. I handed it to Stuart Bradshaw to dispose of, along with the saxophone. Together they made a lovely opportunity for blackmail. I wonder now how I could have been so careless."

Jarrod looked down at his hands, a worried frown forming on his heavy features. "What are you going to do with it now?" The large hands clenched.

"Would it set your mind at rest if I were to destroy it? Yes, I can see it would." He opened the plastic container again and withdrew the cassette. Then he frowned. He rubbed his thumb over the paper label on one side, turned it over and repeated the operation on the second side. Digging his finger nail under the edge of the first label he proceeded to lift it away from the outer surface of the cassette. Jarrod watched in quiet fascination.

Mr Schaeffer suddenly whistled. "Well I'll be — "

"What is it?"

"It seems I seriously underestimated Mr Bradshaw's devious mind. What did he say? Small and incriminating? This is like Pass the Parcel: peel away one layer — "

"What is it?" Jarrod demanded again.

Mr Schaeffer held up a tiny photographic negative. "This is the cleverest bit of all." His voice contained an unaccustomed note of admiration. "How long had he been planning this?"

He stood up and Jarrod leaned forward, expecting to be shown the small celluloid strip. Mr Schaeffer ignored the outstretched hand and deposited the negative in the fire. "Better you don't see," he said quietly.

"You're not a very trusting man, are you?" Jarrod observed.

"Not so as you'd notice."

They both laughed.

For a brief moment the film retained its old image: an upstairs room containing a table and six chairs; and on the table the body of a young man.

Then it flamed and was gone.

Chapter Fourteen

Winter.

In the space of a week it had arrived. There was a brittleness in the air and a new quality in the daylight.

Simon was up late. He pulled back the bedroom curtains. The back lawn was white with frost, and over it the tracks of birds crossed and weaved like stitches on white denim. The sun cast a warm beam low on the ground, making long, grey shadows. It cleft tree trunks in two: black side, bright side. Further down the road the white eaves of houses were glowing.

The frost must have been heavier still when his parents woke, for already the ground mist had risen to the level of the tree tops, cushioning a pink and orange sky. Beneath the mist birds flew, the only movement in a static scene. He knew it must be cold out there, but behind the window, in the full glare of the sun, his skin felt warm.

His head was healing well; the stitches had already been taken out and the wound was now covered with new hair. Apart from cloudy patches of memory that obstinately refused to clear, his brain also seemed to be functioning healthily. But still there was something not right.

At first he had hated the man who had attacked him. For the injuries Simon had suffered — yes; but more for what he had done to Appy. The fact that both men remained at large served to fuel that hatred. But only for a while. Simon found such a violent emotion difficult to sustain; it was not in his nature. Soon he began to feel something else: that he himself was responsible. If only he had done things differently, he told himself, Appy would be alive. He spent long hours reconstructing events in his head, like a losing chess player analysing every error.

Of course, his parents had noticed. They tried to help. As he was off school for a while longer it was possible to go out more, but he tended to stay in the house. He had developed a desire for silence: for sitting alone and watching, thinking. The only time he'd really communicated with people was during the several visits from the police, and even then he'd said no more than was necessary.

Simon dressed methodically. Last night he could not sleep for thinking of today, and now it had finally arrived he couldn't wake up. He knotted the old black tie his father had put out for him and went downstairs.

When he entered the kitchen he could see from the breakfast things that his father had already left. His mother was doing some washing-up. "Your dad's gone to work on the bus today," she said. "He's left the car for us."

Simon sat at the table. He managed half a bowl of cornflakes and a cup of tea. His mother watched him but said nothing.

The drive up to the crematorium was straight and long, leading directly to the chapel at the centre. There was a hearse pulling away as Mrs Bennett parked the car. They were early. The previous funeral must only just have started.

Simon sat and stared through the windscreen at the sweeping lawns and small plots scattered with flowers in various stages of decay. "Come on," his mother said. "Let's go for a walk while we're waiting."

They left the car and walked slowly along the main avenue. At the end, Mrs Bennett turned left towards an archway in a high wall. Beyond was a small rose garden; secluded. There was a bench in the centre. She crossed to it.

"Sit down for a moment," she said.

Simon sat obediently and looked at the surrounding walls. Set into them were little plaques, each carved with a name and dates.

"You never knew your grandad. He died soon after you were born, in a road accident. We decided at the time it was easiest not to tell you." She pointed to one of the plaques near where two walls met. "He was a very keen gardener — loved roses. It seemed the right place."

Simon turned to her. "Why didn't you bring me here before?"

She smiled to herself. "Because it was hard to share it with anyone. I couldn't put it into words, what I felt about him and how he died." She put her hand on Simon's. "It's still not easy. I used to come up here by myself. Then, one day I decided I'd rather remember him as he was when he was alive, not stare at a piece of wall and think of him dying." She squeezed Simon's hand. "It's much better that way."

Together they stood and made their way back to the arch in the wall. Simon took a last look at the garden, its rose bushes dead until Spring.

"Thank you," he said.

*   *   *

The inside of the chapel was sombre and furnished with heavy, dark wood. It was a functional place. The service was short; even so, Simon found it difficult to concentrate. He kept thinking of Appy sitting in his cluttered office brewing a cup of tea, and then of the body in the coffin. He could not make the two images fit, however hard he tried. He did not see the curtains close around the coffin. It had gone before he realised.

They left the chapel and walked to the car. Simon looked up at the sky.

Already the sun was gaining in strength.